Stephen Bignell

Lower Than Angels

Grosvenor House
Publishing Limited

This book is published by
Grosvenor House Publishing Ltd
Link House
140 The Broadway, Tolworth, Surrey, KT6 7HT.
www.grosvenorhousepublishing.co.uk

This book is a work of fiction. Any resemblance to
people or events, past or present, is purely coincidental.

A CIP record for this book
is available from the British Library

ISBN 978-1-80381-300-4

LOWER THAN ANGELS

A NOVEL BY STEPHEN BIGNELL

'YOU MADE THEM A LITTLE LOWER THAN THE ANGELS; YOU CROWNED THEM WITH GLORY AND HONOUR, AND SET THEM OVER THE WORKS OF THY HANDS'

NEW TESTAMENT: Hebrews 2:7

'IN VICTORY, WE WERE ONLY A LITTLE LOWER THAN THE ANGELS'

AN OLD CRICKETER – TUMBLEDON CRICKET CLUB 1778

ENGLAND 1953

England had been at peace for eight years: eight years of austerity and rationing. The Attlee Labour government had given way again to the country's wartime saviour – Winston Churchill. Now a young queen had ascended the throne: a new Elizabethan age was dawning.

With the yoke of war gratefully discarded, the people flocked back to sport: attendances at football and cricket matches reached a new peak. By 1953, anything seemed possible. After 28 attempts, the country's best-known jockey, Gordon Richards, finally rode a Derby winner. At Wembley in May, 38-year-old Stanley Matthews at last won an FA Cup winner's medal with Blackpool.

And now the Australian cricketers were coming back to England to fight for 'The Ashes' once again, for the first tour since 1948, but this time they would be without their indomitable champion Don Bradman.

Not that any of this meant very much to the inhabitants of the neighbouring villages of Rotting Hill and West Rotting, as they prepared to clash in their annual cricket fixture. Historically bitter rivals, the two teams meet in an atmosphere of hostility and antagonism, culminating in an extraordinary denouement.

This is intended to be a novel not about cricket, but about cricketers, and the way the game takes over and dominates their lives. The above villages are mythical, as is the area in which they are located.

The year 1953 marked the watershed between cavalier sportsmanship and a more professional age, but cricket on the village green will hopefully never change; the last bastion of old England that disappeared after the Second World War, but the mere playing of the game continues to spark emotions far beyond its own importance in the grand scheme of things.

Such is our story.

Stephen Bignell
August 2022

Dedicated to the memory of
Denis Charles Scott Compton (1918-1997)

Middlesex, Arsenal, and England

Chapter One

January 6th

JACK

It was a winter's day that hung heavily on the soul; dark, wet, and bitterly cold, the kind of chill that, assisted by a brisk north-easterly wind, could freeze a person in their tracks. It was not a day to be out, but an old man and a sad dog shuffled stiffly down the country lane that skirted the village of West Rotting.

On one side of the lane was a row of trees, their bare branches seeming to shiver in the wind. Beyond them was a field of sheep, though few of them wanted to stray far from their shelter. On the other side of the lane, partly bounded by a hedge, was the cricket ground. The gate was locked now but the sign upon it, badly in need of some retouching, bore the design:

West Rotting Cricket Club – Private Property

Spectators Welcome

The old man and the dog paused, as they did every day at the same spot, as if to pay homage. The ragged hound sniffed around a bit, then looked enquiringly up to his master. Sensing this, the man returned his gaze. 'Aye, Sootcliffe, there's nowt so sad as cricket ground in t'winter.'

Jack's old bones shivered as his tired eyes surveyed the scene once more. It was true, the old ground did look shabby and uncared for. The hallowed square of pitches had been clumsily roped off, but inside the grass glistened green, frosty, and unkempt. Come the spring, Dangerfield the groundsman would begin work on them, and occasionally Jack and Sutcliffe would join him for a chat as he mowed and rolled the precious turf. In the far corner of the ground, the scoreboard stood blank and bleak, with no white numbers visible to telegraph the state of play; locked away for the winter, like the game itself.

Jack looked around to the shaded tree by the boundary where he and Sutcliffe would sit on those sunny summer afternoons and banter cricket with his pal, the Colonel, or any other locals who happened by. The old pavilion was also closed and boarded up, though occasionally the venerable Dangerfield would open it to ensure all was well, dust things down a bit, and apply a lick of paint in the spring. The wooden benches around the ground sat empty and the shaky sightscreens, past their best and bowing to the wind, creaked in the distance. Nothing could be further from the gay scenes of June, July, and August.

It all made the old man sigh. He was tired and lonely, a northerner cast adrift in the southern heartland, with only his melancholy dog and daughter-in-law for company in his little cottage on the north side of the village. His family were all gone now; his two brothers killed on the Somme, and his only son drowned at sea in the more recent war. His friends were left in graves back in Picardy, and his wife had passed away in 1945 from a broken heart. Mary, his son's young bride, was a southern girl who had moved back home to be near her own family and brought Jack with her to care for. It was the least she could do. There was nowhere else for him to go.

"Ome, Sootcliffe,' he murmured. 'No point in stayin' 'ere. Nice warm fire; nice cup o' tea.'

Sutcliffe shot his master a mournful glance, thinking no doubt that he been snoozing nicely in front of the fire before being dragged out for a walk in all this freezing slush and mud. It would take hours for his paws to dry. The gloomy pair ambled off down the lane, Jack casting a last backwards glance at the field of dreams, the one thing that made his dreary life worthwhile.

*

The year was 1953 and the Australians were coming, and for the first time since 1930 there would be no Don Bradman with them. The little master of the willow had retired after the successful 1948 tour of England.

That 1948 side was rated the best Australian team of all time. They had beaten England easily in all three Test series since the war, but it had been a war in which they had suffered little of the deprivations of the mother country. Things were still bleak; rationing would still last for another year, but England was slowly recovering. There was a new queen on the throne; the dawn of a new Elizabethan age.

It had been a time of great austerity, but there was something in the air, something stirring, but still out of reach, out of touch. Old Jack could sense it, a new optimism, something wonderful about to happen. The old country was slowly coming to life again, but not quite yet. It was dark and cold, and the summer was still a long way off.

Chapter Two

August 19th

REG

Reginald George Barclay was going 'over the top'. The date was the first of July 1916. The first day of what became known as 'The Battle of the Somme'. It was a beautiful morning, bright and sunny. In the forward trenches, the British Tommies waited for the signal to go, tense but expectant. For seven days the British guns had pounded the German positions, blown them from their shelters, torn apart the barbed wire. Nothing could have possibly lived through such a bombardment. Their orders were to advance slowly and not to rush. It would simply be a case of walking over no man's land and taking possession of the enemy trenches.

The signal came: the soldiers poured up and over into the open, cheering heartily but not too loudly. It would be a piece of cake. Suddenly Reg could hear shells bursting all around him, the distant deadly chatter of machine-guns. He looked about and saw he was alone, all alone as hell broke loose.

'Wake up, dear,' said Doreen Barclay, swiftly drawing open the bedroom curtains. Reg sat up and rubbed his eyes, passing wind as he did so – a loud, crisp, but odourless blast. 'I wish you wouldn't do that, dear,' said his wife, trying to show disapproval. 'It's not very nice.'

'An empty house is always better than a bad tenant,' observed Reg, grinning at his own adroitness.

'Yes, dear,' replied Doreen, 'and you were talking in your sleep again.'

'Dreaming about Uncle Horace,' said Reg, reaching for his spectacles. 'I always do that when something big is about to happen. Did I ever tell you about Uncle Horace? Killed on the first day of the Somme. Dad never really got over it. They were very close.'

'At least a million times,' murmured Doreen. Her husband ignored her, or he did not hear. 'So, what's so important about today then?'

'Good God, woman!' Reg dragged himself out of bed and began to search for his clothes. 'England need just 94 runs to win the Ashes, and they've got nine wickets in hand. We can't possibly lose now. It'll be a landmark day for English cricket. Nineteen years we've waited for this; 19 sodding years! I've got to be there, can't afford to miss a minute of it. What time is it?'

Doreen watched her husband uneasily as he dressed himself awkwardly, feeling a strange emptiness inside. Reg had never been what you would call handsome, but he had once been attractive to her in an academic sort of way. Lately, however, she thought he had been showing definite signs of going to seed. His once shaggy hair was slowly disappearing, in direct contrast to his waistline, which seemed to be expanding daily. His thick curls – what was left of them – and his even thicker glasses, made him now look like an overgrown schoolboy, which in essence he was. Since they'd married 15 years ago, Reg had never taken that much interest in her, at least not in a physical sense, always being immersed in his cricket, his toy soldiers, and his trains. There had rarely been anything left over for her.

'Sorry, dear, what did you say?' she sighed.

'It doesn't matter, the alarm clock says it's ten past eight. I'd better get my skates on. Breakfast ready yet? Have you made the sandwiches? Come to think of it, probably won't need them. Should be all over by lunchtime. Hope it doesn't rain. Not raining, is it? Doesn't matter anyway, they'll play to a finish whatever. There must be a winner. All the other Tests were drawn, you see, but this one can't be, do you understand? Nineteen bloody years!'

Doreen watched her husband scuttle off to the bathroom, seeming so happy, so full of excitement and anticipation, and she wondered why she never felt like that about anything any more. All she had to enjoy these days was pottering about in her little garden. Sitting down on the bed, she looked at herself in the mirror, the latest perm going grey at the edges. *Not much to look at*, she thought. *No wonder no-one ever notices me, especially Reg, so long as I'm there to cook his meals and iron his shirts*. Her thin features seemed even thinner on reflection; no man would ever look at her twice again; no man would ever want her.

Picking up a tissue from the bedside table, she blew her nose and wandered downstairs to cook the breakfast.

Reg had three great passions in his life, but sadly, Doreen was not one of them. In order of importance, they were:

1. Cricket
2. Military History
3. Railway Trains

The last was a legacy of his youth, which had never really left him. On his days off, Reg would purchase a one-way ticket to London, where he would then buy a 'Red Rover' ticket, enabling him to take buses and visit every London rail terminus, from Victoria and Waterloo in the south to King's Cross, St. Pancras, and Euston in the north, then perhaps to Marylebone and Paddington going west. Thence he would go armed with a notebook and a pencil, together with a duffle bag containing a thermos of tea and a box of sandwiches. There he could be found on the end of some platform or other, along with all the other 'spotters' noting down all the steam locomotive numbers, in a world of his own, scarcely acknowledging the presence of other human beings. On reaching home of an evening, after having eaten, he would sit down at the dinner table, pull out his small volume containing the complete list of all engine numbers, and taking up a red pencil and a ruler, underline the number of any locomotive he had newly 'spotted', occasionally exclaiming, 'Oh good, that's a cop,' or 'Two streaks today; only need another four.'

Doreen, in the armchair, would busily carry on with her knitting, and murmur, 'That's nice, dear,' not having the faintest idea what he was talking about.

When the railway books had been put away, Reg would disappear upstairs to his den and play with his toy soldiers, of which he had a fine collection, along with his many military books. The Barclays had a long history as a martial family; Reg's great-great-grandfather had held the line at Waterloo, his great uncle had served in South Africa, and he could date back some of his ancestors to the French wars of the fourteenth century. It was the one great regret of his life that he himself had not been allowed to serve his country, having been diagnosed as myopic. The field army might have rejected him in 1940, but his short-sightedness did not prevent him working in counterintelligence, where he had become one of the famous 'codebreakers' at Bletchley Park.

Doreen was at least grateful that she had finally persuaded her husband to purchase a television set, so she had something to do when he was playing soldiers. It was so much more interesting than listening to the wireless. They were one of the few households in West Rotting that had a set, and as often as not, her best friend Daphne would come over and they would watch together.

But Reg's overriding passion was undoubtedly cricket. He had never aspired to being a great player, unlike his late father, who was something of a legend at Rotting Hill Cricket Club. Reg had joined the team as a schoolboy, though never rising higher than the 2nd XI. After the war, the club only ran one team, so Reg usually got in the side, but what he lacked in ability he more than made up for by his administrative qualities. At various times he had been club secretary, fixture secretary, and treasurer, and on occasion all three at once, but his greatest pride was that of being the club statistician and archivist – a role he inherited from his father. Reg held all the records of all the teams and all the scores from the beautifully leather-bound scorebooks since the foundation of Rotting Hill Cricket Club in 1859.

The perfectly completed and preserved scoring books had been administered by a succession of immaculate scorers, the latest of which was his wife's best friend, Daphne Charters. Not only had Reg attended every fixture, home and away, since 1930, apart from the war years, but he could recall the result of every game, not to mention the batting scores of individual players, thereby becoming the club 'oracle'. West Rotting Cricket Club had become his life and all-consuming passion.

In a desperate attempt to gain some of her husband's attention, Doreen had volunteered to do the match-day catering, which took up most of her weekends – not that she ever got much thanks for it, at least not from Reg. However, it did mean she could spend more time with her only true friend, Daphne. Doreen had already begun planning for the following Sunday's fixture, which would be against their local village rivals Rotting Hill. This was always the climax of the season – the big 'Gala' match. Just about everyone from the villages would be there, and she needed to put on an especially good show. For all her limitations, the one thing Doreen excelled at was cooking, or in this case, preparing teas for the cricketers. It was, after all, not that demanding, just heaps of bread and filling for the sandwiches, plus some cakes, and gallons of tea and orange juice. This time, however, she wanted to put on something special so that even Reg might notice.

*

In a state of mounting excitement and anticipation, Reg waited anxiously for the bus to take him to nearby Tumbledon to catch his railway connection to London. The rickety old coach made only four round trips a day, five on Saturdays. It was late. Perspiring in the early morning sunshine, Reg alternated between glancing at his watch and peering down the road in the direction from which the bus would be coming. A pair of old ladies waiting at the bus stop, sitting patiently in the adjacent shelter, eyed him strangely as he muttered away to himself, 'Come on, come ON!'

When in a state of nervous excitement, Reg's spectacles would continuously slide down the bridge of his nose, after which he would habitually push them back up again. Like most obsessives, he was totally unaware he was doing this, and after a while began to pace up and down restlessly, cursing under his breath. In normal circumstances, he would have driven his motor car to Tumbledon Station, as he did each day going to work in London. Sadly, his old Austin had broken down just when he needed it most. *Bloody typical!* he thought to himself. His nervous state was becoming so acute that the two old dears in the bus shelter were on the verge of scuttling away, convinced there was a madman on the loose, when eventually the old coach slowly motored into view.

'About bloody time!' complained Reg, much to the consternation of the old biddies, who immediately shrank back even further into the bus shelter. He bounded onto the bus and hurriedly paid his fare, becoming more irritated as the venerable driver took his time searching out the change and producing the ticket. Then he dived for the nearest empty seat, only for another hold-up to ensue as one of the timid ladies proceeded to fumble around in her purse for the bus fare.

By the time the old vehicle chuntered into life once more, poor Reg was almost at boiling point – a condition not helped by the fact that the driver, who must have been 70 if he was a day, pootled along the country lanes as if he had all the time in the world, pulling up at every stop regardless of whether any passengers wished to board or alight. At one point, he even stopped to chat to a farmer in a tractor coming the other way. The two old ladies had taken seats as far away from Reg as possible, and now other passengers on the bus, though few, were also beginning to be concerned about Reg's odd behaviour.

Finally, Reg could bear it no longer and, rising to his feet, lurched to the front of the bus to confront the driver.

'Now look here, my good man, can you please get a move on? I have a train to catch at ten past nine. I have most important business in London and must not, under any circumstances, be late. Do you understand?'

Reg had used his best Foreign Office tone of voice, the authoritative one, the one that threatened to send in a gunboat if the natives didn't stop revolting. The rest of the passengers began to sink lower in their seats.

'Now, 'old yer 'orses, ol' son,' sighed the driver, adjusting his spectacles. 'My eyesight ain't what it used to be, and you can't afford not to be careful in these parts. Now jus' go an' sit down, there's a good chap. We don't want no trouble.'

'Now, look,' bristled Reg, 'I'm going to London to see the Test Match. Do you have any idea of the significance of this! If I don't get there early, I won't get in. Today is the most important day in the history of English cricket, and you're pottering about around these country lanes like you're on some bloody sightseeing tour! When I get to Tumbledon, I'm going to complain to the Inspector. This service is a disgrace!'

The old man gave Reg a meaningful glare, accompanied by some irritated coughing from the rest of the bus. 'Now look, ol' son, jus' calm yerself, you're upsetting the passengers, see? An' it ain't no use complainin', 'cause I am the Inspector. Normal driver called in sick, see, so I 'ad to take over the reins las' minute see, otherwise they'd be no service at all, an' these poor ladies couldn't get to town to do their weekly shoppin'. Now, I'm doin' me best, but I ain't too sure of the route, 'cause it's a long time since I've driven a bus, so I'll get you there as quick as I can. Now, jus' sit down, please.'

Still seething, not to mention feeling slightly chastised, Reg did as he was told. He sensed the eyes of all the passengers were on him, and consequently felt slightly embarrassed. He sat in silence as the old bus bumbled slowly on, continuously glancing at his wristwatch in agitation and pushing his glasses up his nose. *I must be there*, he thought to himself. *I just must, having seen all three days of the match so far and haven't missed a ball. I took a week off work specially. There is no way I can miss the climax. This is the greatest day in English cricket since they won back The Ashes at The Oval in 1926. I remember my dad telling me about it, all the emotion, all the excitement. I must be there!*

Happily, for Reg, at that moment, the old bus climbed to the top of Campden Hill and the ancient market town of Tumbledon flowed into view. To the left was the rolling valley of Grand Farthing Dale, where history claimed the earliest and best-known of time-honoured cricket clubs – Tumbledon. The ancient historic field was deserted now, though the occasional match still took place, despite its former glory having long since faded. The sight of the famous old field always brought a lump to Reg's throat, and for a moment he forgot his impatience; even the bus seemed to pick up speed as it rolled down the gently sloping road into the town.

Within a few minutes, it had pulled up at the railway station, Reg hurtling out through the door, elbowing other passengers out of the way without a word or by-your-leave. Fortunately, he had purchased his train ticket the previous evening – ever meticulous at planning in advance – which was just as well, since his train was on the platform waiting to depart.

As the guard's whistle blew and the steam engine burst into life, Reg breathlessly dived through the nearest door and slumped into a seat. He had made it – just! Still puffing loudly, he failed to notice one of his fellow passengers was Colonel Bartington-Phypps, the Honorary Vice-President of West Rotting Cricket Club.

The old boy, stiff and sitting erect, as one might expect from a former Guardsman, was sporting his usual blood-and-sand M.C.C. tie. 'Hello, Reg old boy, off to The Oval? Great day, eh?' His grey moustache seeming to bristle with excitement as he spoke, perched on the edge of his seat, leaning on his ever-present shooting stick, dressed impeccably as if for a business meeting, though he had retired several years ago.

'I bloody well hope so!' exclaimed Reg. 'Only just made it in time. Useless bus service.'

'Got my daughter to drive me,' confirmed the Colonel. 'Here in plenty of time.'

'Alright for you.' Reg pointed to the old boy's tie. 'You can stroll in whenever you like. I must queue up with the riff-raff. Nearly didn't get in yesterday!'

'Ah yes, useful being a member of the M.C.C. Open doors, you know.'

Yes, I bet it does, privileged bastards, thought Reg, still blowing deeply.

'You alright, old man?' enquired the Colonel.

'How do you think it will go?' Reg's favourite response to a question was always to ask one in reply.

'In the bag by lunchtime, I should think. Bad show Hutton running himself out like that, last evening. Stupid thing to do, but then, what do you expect from a professional captain? And a Yorkshireman at that!'

Silly old buffer, thought Reg. *You wouldn't say that in front of your mate Jack, sitting in our cricket ground.* He suspected the old boy was a bit of a phoney and hadn't seen the fighting he always claimed to have done. In fact, if push came to shove, most of the West Rotting Club were phonies.

Deep down, he detested all these old reactionaries like Bartington-Phypps, who proudly wore his World War I campaign medals, though a nasty rumour going about suggested he had picked them up in an antique shop and had been nothing more than a captain, invalided out of the army after a training accident, before ever seeing a shot fired in anger. Still, he was stuck with the old chap's company for the next half an hour, so he might as well make the most of it.

After a brief silence, Reg suggested, 'We've still got nine wickets to go, and the Aussies don't have the spinners with the ability of Lock and Laker. With our batsmen like Edrich and Compton, plus young May and Graveney, I don't see how we can fail. Then, if the worst comes to the worst, there's still old Barnacle Bailey to fall back on.'

'Good point, Reg,' said the Colonel, stroking his bushy moustache. 'Edrich and Compton should see us through. Do you know, Edrich was a bomber pilot during the last dust-up? Flew Lancasters, I believe. Stared death in the face every day. Need a man like that on your side. Good old British bulldog, just like Winnie, eh? Not so sure about Compton, though. Bit of a showman, if you want to know. Gives his wicket away too easily. Gammy leg, so I heard. Didn't see much service, by all accounts. Nice soft posting as a P.E. Instructor out east. Doubt if he saw any action at all.'

Ignorant git, thought Reg. *Probably saw about as much action as you did*. If there hadn't been women in the carriage, he would have told him so.

Thankfully, the Colonel changed the subject. 'Playing Sunday, Rotting Hill, isn't it?'

Reg's mood perked up at the question. 'Hope to be. Hope to be. One or two players on holiday, so we're scratching around a bit. Still, shouldn't be a problem. Those peasants haven't beaten us since before the war.'

The old boy leaned forward earnestly. 'Don't underestimate them. Heard they'd been doing reasonably well this year. Beat Tumbledon Thirds, so I believe, not to mention Beech Cross.'

'That's not much form,' Reg scoffed. 'Everyone beats Beech Cross, and Tumbledon 3s are nothing but pensioners and schoolboys.'

The Colonel sat stiffly in his seat, impassively leaning on his stick, his hands clasped together as if in prayer. It was the pose he always adopted when sitting on the bench under the big oak tree in the cricket ground, where he and his crony Jack Hurst could be found every match day. The old soldier sat thoughtfully for a few moments, whilst his younger companion gazed out of the window. As ever on train journeys, Reg had brought his trainspotter's notebook with him, but felt somewhat embarrassed to take it out in such company.

'Got a point, old boy,' spoke the Colonel at length, 'but they've got one or two useful players. That young Stewart boy is a bit brisk.'

'Huh! If they can keep him off the booze for long enough. Did you know he drove his father's combine harvester into a ditch the other day? Got hushed up, though. No witnesses. Pater's got a lot of influence, being a Justice of the Peace and all that.' Reg sniffed and carried on looking out of the window.

After that, the two men did not speak until the train reached Clapham Junction, where they both alighted to catch the electric train to Vauxhall, losing touch in the milling crowd of expectant cricket fans.

Reg began to feel apprehensive again as a mad rush to the ground followed, quietly cursing at the long queues stretching around the famous Kennington Oval. It seemed like the whole of England was there. He patiently waited his turn along with everyone else, despite feeling inwardly frantic. Thankfully, just before play was due to start, he squeezed through a turnstile and was in the celebrated old arena, scene of so many historic triumphs, though somewhat dilapidated now since the war.

The first ever Test Match in England had been played there, way back in 1880, when the legendary W.G. Grace scored 152 and England won by five wickets. Two years later, amidst unbearable tension, Australia had won by seven runs. Shortly afterwards, the famous obituary notice for English cricket appeared in *The Times* newspaper, and the legend of 'The Ashes' was born. There, in 1926, England won them back after a long wait, as both Hobbs and Sutcliffe hit centuries in England's second innings. That year, like the present one, the first four Tests had been drawn, and the series rested on the final game at The Oval. In 1938, with Europe on the brink of another war this century, a 22-year-old Yorkshireman named Leonard Hutton had scored a record 364, as England piled up 903 for 7 and won by an innings. In the last Ashes game played there, England had been skittled out for 52, and the great Don Bradman was bowled for a duck in his final Test innings. Such memories!

The game got underway amidst an air of great tension and excitement. Reg was squashed on a bench seat on the popular side, irritatingly next to some noisy schoolchildren, but so engrossed in the match that they hardly registered.

The weather was set fair, but the Australians, aware of the implications of their defeat, fought every inch of the way, every English run having to be hard earned. The England overnight batsman, Edrich and May, dug in, and for a while the crowd went very quiet, the silence being so loud, and the tension so great, that one scarcely dared to breathe. Runs were greeted with polite applause and occasional cheering. Slowly they came; ever more slowly. The rare hit to the boundary was met with a momentary lift in the mood of the massive throng.

With the score at 88, with 44 runs still needed, young May was brilliantly caught by Davidson at square leg. A future England captain, he departed to respectful applause.

But now, Denis Compton entered the arena to join his Middlesex teammate; the 'Terrible Twins', as they became known, back together again. In the golden summer of 1947, the pair had scored over 7000 runs between them for the country and county, lifting the hearts of all English men and women, weary from so many years of war and hardship. Though close to being past their best, they were still great batsmen, still hearts of oak, the yeomen of England, the legacy of the men who had stood at Agincourt and Waterloo. They would surely see it through.

When the lunch interval was taken, England had reached 108 for 2 wickets, with just 24 needed for victory. Unable to move from his seat, Reg wolfed down his sandwiches, drank his tea from the thermos flask, now almost cold, and fidgeted about until the match resumed 40 minutes later.

As each run was ticked off, the spirit of the crowd began to rise. Outside in the streets. traffic came to a stop as passengers crammed into the tops of buses to catch a glimpse of history about to be made. Around the country, all England was listening on their wireless sets, or watching for those lucky enough to own televisions. Factories came to a standstill, and office workers put down their pens and huddled around the nearest radio.

Then, shortly before three o'clock, Morris bowled, and Compton swept the ball to the boundary. Before the ball reached the ropes, it had disappeared into the milling, cheering throng that flooded onto the field. Tears streaming down his cheeks, Reg was swept along until he stood with the crush beneath the players' balcony, calling for three cheers.

For more than an hour, engulfed by what seemed half of England, Reg stood on the hallowed turf, listening to the speeches and calling for the victors one by one: Len Hutton, the country's first professional captain this century; the old war hero Bill Edrich, who had defied everything the opposition had thrown at him; Graveney, May, and Trueman – the young hopefuls; Laker and Lock – the spin twins that had made victory possible the day before; Godfrey Evans – the jovial livewire wicketkeeper; Trevor Bailey who, along with Willie Watson, had rescued a lost cause at Lord's back in June; the veteran Alec Bedser – the best bowler on either side; and lastly, Denis Compton. It was fitting that he should score the winning runs after being on the losing side against the Aussies so many times.

To Reg, they were heroes all. It was the greatest day of his life; like the whole country had been reborn. When almost everyone had left the celebrations, he remained standing there in front of the famous old pavilion, long after all the cheering had died, his cheeks still moist. Eventually, a kindly policeman ushered him away, and he slowly left the ground, continually turning around to gaze back at the scene of triumph, as if the leaving of it would make the day's events seem like a dream, that it hadn't really happened.

Outside in the streets, people were waving flags, singing, and dancing, Union Jacks hanging from the windows of nearby houses. Reg wandered about, not really knowing where he was walking, drinking it all in for what seemed hours. It felt like the whole country was having a party, but he was an outsider, not invited in. By some chance, he finally found himself at the railway station. Happy and weary, it was time for him to go home, back to dreary old Doreen and his humdrum life. But what a day!

Chapter Three

August 20th

THE BLACK PIG

There had been a settlement at Rotting Hill dating back to Roman times. The area was mentioned in the Domesday Book, and a substantial village had existed since the Middle Ages, but all that now remained from the medieval era was the old Norman church of St. Stephen.

The district had changed considerably in Victorian times, and a once prosperous farming community had been slowly run down during the Industrial Revolution. A few farms remained, but most of the inhabitants were now commuters, either to London or the nearby town of Tumbledon.

During the railway boom of the mid-nineteenth century, a branch line had run from Tumbledon, through Rotting Hill and West Rotting, to Beech Cross and Woodhurst, but had fallen into disuse long before nationalisation. Consequently, the village was somewhat cut off from civilisation, with only two buses a day passing through. Because of this, Rotting Hill had become neglected and something of a rural outpost, its inhabitants detached and parochial, but nevertheless retaining a strong sense of togetherness and resentment to the world outside, now often being regarded as the poor relations of the area.

There was some dichotomy as to how the name of the village originated; some claiming it came from the fact that, during Roman occupation, the inhabitants had been massacred in reprisal for the murder of a local magistrate, with the corpses left unburied at the top of the hill as a warning to other potential rebels. Another party argued that the name derived from the deer that once roamed the nearby woods, and the cries that echoed across the valley from the male bucks during the rutting season.

One thing that was for sure, was from the top of Rotting Hill, one could stand in three counties almost at the same time. The village itself, which lay at the foot of a gentle slope, was officially in Sussex, while the nearby village of West Rotting, two miles to the north-west, was administered by the county of Surrey. Then, only a few hundred yards to the east of the village, was the border with Kent.

The consequence of this confusion was that Rotting Hill came under the auspices of Sussex County Council, who, disputing that the village was under their jurisdiction, refused for many years to even acknowledge its existence. The upshot of all this was that the villagers ran their own affairs as an autonomous community and resented any outside interference when it did come.

Little now remained of the original settlement. In the centre of the village was a large pond, somewhat stagnant, bordered by a small green on one side and a row of old buildings on the other. The buildings included an inn, called The Black Pig, a small grocery shop, which doubled as a post office, and the village hall, adjacent to the church of Saint Stephen. A row of cottages stood on the road that ran up the hill, eventually swinging left in the direction of West Rotting, with a considerably larger number of residential buildings on the flatter ground as the same road pointed east towards Wychurst and Tumbledon.

The landlord of The Black Pig was Hubert – known to all as 'Bert' – Fisher, who ran the place with his daughter Hazel. He had previously owned a pub in the Elephant and Castle district of London, but, sick of being bombed out, had moved to Rotting Hill in 1943 when the previous landlord had suddenly died, leaving no known relatives. Bert picked up the place for a song, and though it made little profit, he and Hazel were content enough after all the hustle and bustle of the big city.

More recently, the pub had been bought up by a brewery chain, and the Hetherington ale served was the envy of the surrounding area. Visitors sometimes drove all the way from Tumbledon just to sample it, but most of the time the tavern was patronised by the usual band of regulars, including the local cricket team which doubled as the darts team in the winter months.

There had once been a cricket pitch in the village, but the ground had been requisitioned during the war for farmland and growing vegetables. The villagers did not have enough money to restore it after the war nor to build a new ground, so from 1946 they decided the only way to keep the team going was to play all their matches away, as a 'wandering' side. To this end, they had acquired a battered old 1930 charabanc to transport the team and its entourage (usually consisting of half the village) to the match venues, the old coach becoming a regular sight at local villages in Sussex and Kent, often the object of much amusement. The cricket team became vital for the camaraderie and self-esteem of the 'Rotting Hillbillies', as the side was sarcastically nicknamed; the one strand that bound them all together.

On the Thursday evening following England's historic triumph over Australia at The Oval, The Rotting Hill cricket team had their usual pre-match meeting in the pub. Unsurprisingly, most of the talk was about the 'Ashes' win, much of which they had watched the previous lunchtime on Bert's television in the lounge of The Black Pig, with many being late back for work, or ostensibly attending a grandmother's funeral! Bert's 'telly' was believed to be the only one in the village and had proved a great attraction on cold winter nights, especially for the ladies, while their menfolk drank in the main bar.

But it was now a balmy summer's evening, and although most of the patrons were sitting outside on the rough wooden benches, Ken Kippax was holding court as usual inside, propping up the bar, chain-smoking, and downing one pint of Hetherington's Ale after another. From the moment he lit his cigarettes, they left his mouth only briefly for a large gulp of beer to pass his lips, as he talked rapidly about many subjects, each of which he claimed to be an expert on. Consequently, by the end of the evening, his clothes would be covered in cigarette ash.

Ken was a tallish man, though slightly stooped, with handsome features and a muscular body that belied his bad habits. He was also almost completely bald but had allowed what was left of the hair on the side of his head to grow, so he could comb it sideways and upwards to partially cover the top of his head. If this was not sad enough, he aggravated the look by smearing huge dollops of hair cream around his head, somewhat indiscriminately, so that in the hot weather it melted and ran down his face.

Legend claimed, though no- one was quite certain from where the story originated, that Ken had been the first man ashore on the Normandy beaches during the D-Day invasion in 1944, suffering an unspecified shrapnel wound which occasionally inconvenienced him, most especially when an opposing batsman was carting his gentle off-breaks all around the park. A staunch trade unionist and member of the Communist Party, he regarded himself as an expert in politics and other serious issues. The cricket club captain, Rupert St. Charles, once described Ken, in his typically whimsical manner, as 'a man of forthright views and fifth-rate opinions'. But he was a good chap to have on your side and long renowned as the spiritual leader of the team, if not the village itself. He was also somewhat prone to exaggeration, as indeed was his lifelong pal and drinking crony, Ted Jolly.

If ever a man's name was less appropriate to his nature, it was Ted. A rotund fellow, by day he worked as a gardener at nearby Grandthorpe Manor, a large country pile owned by Rupert's eccentric, crotchety old mother, Lady Edwina St. Charles. As the evenings wore on, Ted would match Ken pint for pint, all the time complaining about everything under God's sun, sometimes waffling away so uncontrollably that everyone in the pub would collapse in fits of laughter. Though both men were in their late forties, Ted's drinking excesses had not been so kind to his waistline. His mousy hair was always cropped short, and the only other distinguishing feature of his permanently glum face was his huge nose, earning him the nickname of 'Beaky'.

Ted was famously the team's wicket keeper, as his lack of mobility prevented him from fielding anywhere else. During a game, he would keep up an incessant diatribe of griping from behind the stumps, cursing everyone from bowlers and fielders, to umpiring decisions, the state of the pitch, and the weather; in fact, everything that annoyed him, which was just about anything. In the course of his duties, he had broken most of his fingers at one time or another.

A third member of the team to join the regular early customers in the bar was Billy Moon, a genial giant of a man with a round, ruddy face, thick hair, and spectacles. He was renowned for being the butt of everyone's jokes, though he was rarely aware of this. He earned his living as an odd-job man about the village, being a jack-of-all-trades, but very definitely a master of none. This motley trio, who normally batted nine, ten, and 11 in the order, were nevertheless the backbone of the team, playing week in, week out; never missing a game.

Hazel Fisher did most of the work behind the bar, whilst her father idled his time away watching the television or chatting to the customers. This evening, Billy had been watching her slightly more than was usual. Hazel seemed aware of this and was trying hard to keep an eye on him without catching his attention.

At 35, she was probably slightly past her best, typically buxom for a barmaid without being physically fat. Her features were not unattractive, adorned with thick, wavy black hair, though she was developing something of a double chin, and her figure was beginning to spread. She had worked as a barmaid for most of her adult life, apart from a brief spell as a bus conductress during the war.

Billy had lusted after her from the very first day she and Bert had appeared in the village to take control of the pub ten years previously, though she had always rebuffed his advances – at least until recently. It was rumoured that she had 'put it about a bit' during the war years, and there were further whispers of one or two liaisons between her and some of the lustier village males, even the local vicar of St. Stephen's – the Reverend Christopher Christian – though Billy opted not to believe any of this. He had helped to renovate the pub on the Fishers' arrival and had fallen in love with her from the start, though she pretended not to be interested in him despite them becoming friends.

For the past few years, Hazel had accompanied the team to their matches on the old bus, as cheerleader and team scorer. Such trips, especially victorious outings, would often end with the entire team spending the evenings celebrating in the local clubhouse and bar, with much loud and hearty singing on the way home. Hazel was a particularly good vocalist, very audible in the Sunday church services.

A few weeks earlier, Billy and Hazel had found themselves sitting together on the coach where, both the worse for drink, they had indulged in what Billy later called 'some serious snogging'. This had escalated the following week at Tumbledon C.C., where the couple had wandered outside for some air and a grope, which got out of hand, ending up in the ground's scorebox, when she had pulled down her drawers and impaled herself on Billy's slightly startled penis, which she had extricated from his trousers with a dexterity that belied her portly frame. In their drunken state, neither party gained much satisfaction from the encounter, though Billy had dined out on the episode ever since. Hazel, however, later felt embarrassed and had been avoiding Billy as far as possible.

As the rest of the team arrived for the scheduled meeting, Hazel brought over a huge plate of sandwiches, hot roasted potatoes, and pies, as was the usual form. Billy made to say something to her, but she ignored him and walked off.

By now, the trio of Ken, Ted, and Billy had been joined by Alf Fortune and Barry Dick, two other team members. Hazel fussed around them all for a while, though she seemed a bit tetchy as Billy eyed her a little too obviously.

Ken could not help noticing this and remarked, 'Asked her for another poke yet?' Billy looked a little sheepish, blushing slightly and rubbing his nose, as he did when agitated.

'Yeah, we heard about you giving her one at the Tumbledon match,' added Ted. 'Why don't you go and see what she's doin' later? You can get another round in while you're at it.'

This was a good manoeuvre, since Billy was notorious for not standing his round and cadging drinks off everyone else, though he always seemed to have plenty of money to spend. Thus compromised, he could now hardly avoid going up to the bar.

'Yeah, I gave 'er a good lookin' at,' boasted Billy, meaning 'a good seeing to', as he had a preponderance to malapropism – a constant source of amusement to his pals.

'More like the other way round,' scoffed Ted.

Reluctantly, Billy wandered off to the bar, groping in his pocket for some money while his mates sniggered behind him. Hazel was absent-mindedly washing some glasses the other side of the bar and cast him only the briefest of glances. Since their recent entanglement, the pair were now somewhat awkward in each other's company.

For once, Billy seemed slightly lost for words, so it was Hazel who broke the uneasy silence. 'Yes, luv, what can I get yer?'

'Er… five pints of Heths, please.' Billy glanced over his shoulder at the grinning faces.

She said, 'Pushing the boat out, are we?' and began pulling the pints, still avoiding his gaze as Billy started to feel somewhat uncomfortable.

This particular night, Hazel was not looking her best. She suddenly appeared distinctly unattractive, more than a little grumpy, and looking dull and rather podgy. Her face was blotchy and pale, her hair wild and in need of a brush. A cigarette, dangling from the side of her mouth as she spoke, only added to the undignified effect. She finally finished pulling the last pint and placed them on a tray.

'Anythin' else, luv?' she sighed.

Billy coughed and whispered, 'Erm… about the other night?'

'What about it?'

'Well, erm… you know, fancy another bunk-up?'

She stared disapprovingly at him, though her distant expression did not change. 'Sorry, dear,' she smiled weakly, 'can't tonight. Got the painters in,' then walked off to serve another customer. Looking totally bewildered, Billy picked up the tray and wandered back to his mates.

'Well, how did you get on?' grinned Ken.

'Things a bit awkward now,' stated Billy, matter-of-factly. 'She's 'avin' 'er room decorated.' Everyone immediately collapsed into fits of laughter.

'What, at this time of night?' chortled Ted.

'Never mind, mate,' giggled Barry, barely able to speak. 'Keep at it.'

'I don't get it,' offered Billy, still looking perplexed. 'I thought I was the only decorator in the village.'

Ken, attempting to suck the froth off his pint, almost choked as he blew the beer head all over the table. Alf Fortune, sitting opposite, took the full force, but creased up laughing. He was a short man, with a jolly red face and stubbly grey hair, the veteran of the team. Known unsurprisingly as 'Lucky', in his life he had been anything but, having drunk and gambled away what little money he had. Now, at the age of 55, he had to seek what menial work he could find.

All through this little scenario, the fifth member of the group, Barry Dick, had been giggling incessantly. In fact, he giggled like a silly schoolgirl, which had the effect of making everyone present laugh even more. Barry – real name Barrimore Garibaldi Dick – was a swarthy, stocky fellow, of unknown pedigree who, during the recent war, had managed to dodge conscription and make a lucrative living selling illicit goods on the black market. The story went that his father was a Scot and his mother an Italian film star. Whatever, they certainly had a sense of humour. Even eight years from the end of the war, his income was a bit of a mystery, as he lived in an old barn on Barker's Farm, a mile out of town, above his so-called 'Antique Shop', that sold everything from silk stockings to second-hand tractors.

Just at that moment, Hazel reappeared with another bowl of hot roasted potatoes. Sensing the ribald atmosphere, she scowled, 'An' what's ticklin' you lot then?' guessing the answer. The sniggering stopped, replaced by knowing smirks all round.

'We hear you're being decorated, Hazel, tee, hee, hee, hee,' piped up Barry.

'Oh, very amusing,' she responded dryly. 'You boys really crease me up.' She gave Billy a withering glance, collected some empty glasses, and wandered off.

Everyone went quiet and looked suitably chastised. Everyone except Billy, still appearing bewildered.

Ken quickly changed the subject. 'Anyone seen Wally? He's usually the first one here.'

''E was,' offered Hazel, reappearing and wiping some beer off the table and picking up some empty plates. ''E's been sittin' outside all evenin' on 'is tod, where you boys should be on a nice night like this, 'stead o' makin' a mess in 'ere.'

'What's he doin' out there, then?' asked Billy.

'Feelin' a bit sorry for 'imself, I shouldn't wonder,' answered Hazel, stopping her wiping and standing up straight with a serious expression. 'So would you be if it was the anniversary of your poor wife passin' away. We was both at the churchyard this mornin' payin' our respects. 'E was still there lunchtime when I come back to do the lunches.'

Walter Richardson's wife Janice had passed away after a long battle with cancer. She and Hazel had been close friends. A deeply religious woman, Janice had been active in the community for many years and was sorely missed. Wally had never really got over it, still living in their little cottage on the outskirts of the village with his memories and his collie dog, Barney, presently curled up at his master's feet, taking in the evening sunshine. Hazel called out to her father to come and mind the bar while she went outside to see them.

'Yeah, I forgot about ol' Wally's missus,' said Alf, his red face getting redder and redder, and the worse for drink already. 'Only a year ago, wannit? Poor ol' Wally, floating like a lonely turd in the lavatory pan of life.'

Ken shot him a queer look. 'Fuck me, Alf, what a homespun philosopher you're turning into!'

'Eh?' queried Billy.

There was a brief silence before Barry piped up, playing devil's advocate, 'So, what exactly did Hazel say to you then, Billy?'

'Eh?'

'About the decorators?'

Billy pondered for a moment, rubbed his nose and replied, 'Oh right, that. I think she said she had the painters in.'

Everyone burst out laughing again, all except poor Billy, looking more bemused than ever.

'Eh? What's so funny then?'

'I believe it's a euphemism for a certain female condition,' explained Ken.

'Eh? What's a "youthism"?' Billy seemed more perplexed than ever.

By now most of the group were laughing so much their ribs were hurting. 'Come on, let's go outside and cheer up Wally,' Ken said, taking the lead as usual. 'I don't think the penny's ever going to drop. Somebody bring the grub.'

'Yeah, let's go outside,' agreed Alf. 'I don't think I can take much more of this.'

They all stumbled out into the warm night air, still laughing, and drawing attention from the other patrons.

Wally was sitting alone on the bench furthest from the door, except for his faithful hound Barney, snoozing underneath. He was a short, lean man, with thinning brown hair and hazel eyes, topped by a pair of eyebrows that appeared too big for his spare face. Barney stirred and let out a doggy groan, annoyed at being disturbed by unwanted company.

'Hi Wally, how's things goin', mate?' greeted Ken in his best bonhomie, sitting down beside him as the others all pitched up noisily onto the bench seats.

'Alright for Sunday?' enquired Alf, for something to say.

It was a pointless question, as Walter Richardson had not missed a game since the war. He had once been a fine opening batsman in his younger days, but latterly his batting had become somewhat ponderous, though he was only 44 and still fit as a fiddle.

'Yeah, I s'pose so,' said Wally, absent-mindedly.

'So, 'oo we got so far then?' asked Alf, pulling out a dingy notebook and pencil from his pocket. He was the team 'organiser', which was something of a misnomer since he was one of the most disorganised persons you would wish to meet. But he had been given that role for the sake of gainful employment, being an ineffective member of the team on the field.

'Right then,' began Ken, 'there's us six, OK? Presumably the Rev's gonna play, then Charlie, and I 'eard his brother Tark's around this weekend, so that's nine.

Anyone seen Charlie, by the way?' As he spoke, his cigarette wiggled up and down in his mouth. Eventually, about an inch of ash fell off, landing on Barney, who let out a stifled growl. 'Sorry, ol' son,' apologised Ken.

'Charlie' was Rupert St. Charles, eldest though sadly disowned son of the 17th Earl of Ashfield, whose family lived in the nearby stately home of Grandthorpe Manor. Rupert was presently the blackest in a long line of family black sheep, having disgraced himself at Cambridge in mid-term by going off to fight for the International Brigade in the Spanish Civil War. On his return to England, he registered himself as a conscientious objector, thereby avoiding conscription in the recent World War. Clearly a man of principle, he now lived in near squalor in a small cottage on the outskirts of the village with his busty Spanish girlfriend, who everyone called 'Carmen', her real name being unpronounceable. Here, Rupert made a living as an artist, sculptor, occasional gardener, and political agitator.

Charlie had always been a useful cricketer, honed at public school and university. And, due to his education and tactical knowledge, he had been elected captain of the team. His younger brother Tarquin was more respectable, 'something in the city', and lived in some splendour in Chelsea. He occasionally visited his family seat, now solely occupied by his mother Edwina, who was dottier than a dalmatian with measles, along with his wayward, socially calamitous sister Olivia, who had had several nervous breakdowns following a series of scandalous affairs. His father Cameron, the Earl, now resided in Barbados, where he was living it up with a harem of dusky mistresses.

The St. Charles family already had a chequered history: originally Norman, and known as Sainte-Charles, they had settled in the area as far back as the 11th century, though remained obscure until the first Earl, Edmund, was granted his title and lands by King Edward III as a reward for service in the Hundred Years War in the 1340s. Thereafter, the family embarked on four centuries of appalling bad luck (or more possibly bad judgement) in continually backing the wrong side in domestic squabbles.

In the 15th century 'Wars of the Roses', the 4th Earl, Clarence, sided first with the Yorkists, then with the House of Lancaster, then finally the Yorkists once again – each new alliance coinciding with a military disaster, culminating in King Richard the Third's defeat at Bosworth in 1485. After that, the family kept a lower profile until the 9th Earl, Edward, opposed Parliament in the English Civil War of the 1640s, which ended with his lands being confiscated by Oliver Cromwell's regime in 1651, though they were later restored by Charles II on the restoration of the monarchy.

By tradition, the St. Charles clan were fiercely Catholic, and were linked with a plot to overthrow Queen Elizabeth the First and usurp her with the imprisoned Mary Stuart, Queen of Scots, – a decision which cost Henry, youngest son of the 7th Earl, his head! A further catastrophe was only just averted in 1745 when the 12th Earl, Strudwick, was persuaded at the last moment to throw in his lot with Bonnie Prince Charlie's Jacobite rebellion.

The military tradition continued, though this time on the right side. Hugo, the 14th Earl, lost both his legs leading a cavalry charge at Waterloo, though this did not prevent him later siring seven children, including Rupert's great-grandfather, Cecil, who rode with the Light Brigade at Balaclava. Sadly, Rupert had reverted to the old family tradition, supporting the Spanish Republicans, though his experiences in that war so traumatised the young noble that he was to remain a pacifist thereafter.

'I saw the Spanish bint earlier,' said Barry, in his usual subtle manner. 'She was cycling up towards Tumbledon.'

'Well, that's no bleedin' good, is it?' returned Ted, who by now had stripped down to his rather shabby vest. 'She doesn't captain this team!'

'I know that, you fat ponce!' parried Barry. 'What's your problem anyway?'

Ted and Barry did not get on, often deliberately antagonising each other. After one recent match, which had been narrowly lost, they had ended up brawling on the dressing room floor and had to be separated by their teammates.

'I might be fat, but I'm not a ponce!' bristled Ted.

'Alright, alright, keep it stowed, lads,' said Ken. 'We're supposed to 'avin' a team meeting before the most important game of the season, half the side haven't even turned up yet, and you two twats are squabbling again. Right, let's call this meeting to order. Anybody got a fag?'

Barry stirred the pot again. 'Look, this isn't one of your trade union meetings.'

'Shut up, knobhead!' ordered Ted.

Barry got to his feet threateningly. 'Make me then!'

Another serious altercation was nipped in the bud by the appearance of the vicar of St. Stephen's, the Reverend Christopher Christian – a tall, blond, well-built man in his mid-thirties, with an almost permanent constipated expression. 'Sorry I'm late, chaps,' he announced gaily. 'Been writing the sermon for Sunday.'

'Dunno why you bother,' said Alf. 'No-one goes to church these days.'

'Well, yes, I've been meaning to talk to you chaps about that.'

'Bunch of 'eathens!' added Hazel, a regular churchgoer nowadays, despite her chequered past. 'Hello, Chris,' she said brightly. 'Pint of the usual, is it?' Everyone couldn't help noticing her mood improving with the appearance of the handsome young vicar. Throwing away her cigarette, she brushed her hair absent-mindedly away from her face. Many believed there were other motives behind her new-found religious zeal.

'Yes, please,' returned Chris. 'Now, about what I was saying earlier—'

'What about Tim?' interrupted Alf, back on selection business.

'Last seen drunk in charge of a combine harvester,' laughed Ken.

''E's bin banned,' stated Hazel matter-of-factly, polishing the table with a wet rag as she continued gazing affectionately at the vicar – something Billy couldn't help noticing. 'Dad barred 'im last week when 'e got so legless 'e fell arse over 'ead and knocked over a table full o' drinks. 'Is ol' man won't let 'im drive any farming stuff any more.'

'Thought I hadn't seen 'im around,' Ken said. 'When was that, then? Don't remember that.'

'Must have been the night of your union meeting,' offered Ted drily.

'He's bin drinking at the White Swan in 'Olly Oak, so I 'eard,' confirmed Alf.

Chris sat down on one of the benches as Hazel brought him his drink, Billy noticing it was the first time he had seen her smile all evening.

He rubbed his nose, shifted awkwardly in his seat, then enquired, 'You playing Sunday, Vic? It's West Rotting.'

'Well, yes, I know,' returned Chris, tilting his head and frowning. His round, almost cherubic face did not sit well with his air of world-weariness. 'I'd really like to play, but I'd also really like you boys to turn up for morning service. Very few of you do, you know.'

'You tell 'em, Chris!' Hazel had remained outside, leaning against the wall behind the benches, gazing admiringly at the young priest.

'Haven't you got some customers to serve?' snapped Billy, rather uncharacteristically.

Hazel's face darkened immediately. 'Well, excuse me!' She shot Billy a withering look, folded her arms, and stormed back inside the pub.

'That was a bit uncalled for,' said Wally, who had kept his counsel all this time, but was clearly annoyed at Billy's rudeness. He was also rumoured to have a soft spot for the barmaid. Getting up, he followed her inside, Barney trotting dutifully after.

'So, that's eight-an'-'alf then,' said Alf, scribbling in his notebook.

'Nine-and-a-half, if you include Tim,' added Ken. 'I'm sure he'll want to play, especially after the punch-up at the darts match.'

The incident to which Ken was alluding had occurred at the Tumbledon and District Darts League match between West Rotting and Rotting Hill the previous March. The local constabulary had been called following a dust-up at the end of evening, when Ken, Tim, and one or two others had taken exception to some of the West Rotting players celebrating a close victory a trifle too vociferously and vindictively.

There had been bad feeling between the two villages for some time, occasionally overspilling onto the cricket field. Rotting Hill had not beaten their neighbours since before the war; the West Rotting players always appearing a little too snobbish and triumphalist for Ken's liking. He dreamed endlessly of downing those 'stuck-up bastards' and being able to gloat himself, though it seemed unlikely to happen, for West Rotting had a very good team and rarely lost to anybody.

However, this year seemed different. Times were changing. Ken sensed it; so did some of the others. England had just won back The Ashes. There was a new queen on the throne. Echoes of the recent war were drifting into silence. The country was looking up again. Its people were getting some pride back. There was hope for the future.

The rest of the evening was spent with the team discussing tactics, such as they were. As more and more ale was consumed, the prognosis for a possible victory on Sunday increased. Whatever happened, it would be a grand occasion. Most of the village would be going along – as many as possible in the old charabanc, but many others would be making their own way there. The weather was set fair; they could not wait to get at them.

As darkness fell, the pub slowly emptied, and by closing time most of the patrons had drifted away, back to their homes. It had been a momentous couple of days, and the anticipation was just beginning.

Chapter Four

August 21st

DAPHNE

Daphne Charters and Doreen Hiscutt had been friends almost from the moment they were born, just two weeks apart, in the autumn of 1915. Their families had lived in the same little terraced street in Tumbledon, which in those days was barely more than a village, and they had attended the same junior and senior schools together. Even then, the pair – always known as 'Daf' and 'Dor' – had been inseparable.

As often is the case in such partnerships, the two pals were totally different in looks and character: Daphne, always a well-proportioned girl, was generous of feature, thought, and nature; whilst Doreen, small, thin, and timid, always seemed to dwell in her shadow. Yet there was never any feeling of domination, Daphne having taken her little pal under her wing from the outset, and that was how it had stayed ever since. When anyone had dared to bully or browbeat her bashful, nervous friend, Daphne would protect Doreen. They had always known they would be lifelong friends.

After leaving school, the girls had both joined the same secretarial college and gone on to work in the Civil Service. In 1938, however, their union was broken when Doreen, after an uncharacteristic and whirlwind romance, had married Reginald Barclay. When the war broke out, the patriotic Daphne had enlisted in the Women's Royal Naval Reserve (known as the WRENS), wherein she served until 1946, whilst Doreen settled down to an unhappy and unfulfilled married life.

The two women had drifted apart, though they always kept in touch, both being avid letter writers. When the war ended, Daphne returned to her secretarial work with local outfitting business Commodore Sports, which happened to be run by Cedric Winford-Harvey, the captain of the West Rotting cricket team. Tragically, both Daphne's parents had been killed in an air raid, so on demob she had bought herself a little cottage in West Rotting, just a hundred yards or so from where the Barclays lived.

Time had not been kind to Daphne. She had spread out from the broad-featured girl of her youth, though she remained a jolly, gregarious sort, who defied her spinster loneliness with a brave smile. Doreen, meanwhile, was just as mousy and miserable as ever, only seeming to cheer up in her friend's company.

Every Friday night, Reg Barclay would attend the Toy Soldiers Modelling Society meeting in Tumbledon, and as he never got back home until late, Daphne would take the opportunity to keep her old friend company for a few hours and have a good natter over a bottle of

Reg's homemade wine. This evening, Daphne was in an especially buoyant mood, in direct contrast to her little pal, who seemed more down in the dumps than ever.

'I say, Dor.' She giggled as Doreen poured out her third glass of the night. 'You're giving the old wine a bit of hammer!'

Doreen appeared not to notice, and said nothing. Her face looked thinner than usual, and specks of grey were appearing amidst her mousy curls.

'I'm a bit upset, if you must know,' she confirmed eventually.

'What's the matter then, my little hamster?' bubbled Daphne, tilting her head sideways like a dog straining to hear a strange sound, her ever jolly smile widening as he did so. Despite her years, she still possessed a beautiful, round, smooth countenance, with lovely green eyes and a big, warm red mouth. Though still quite attractive to men, Daphne had now settled into a spinster's life, with no ambition of marriage.

Doreen was looking somewhat distressed. 'I don't know if I can really talk about it.'

'Oh, come on, Dor, you can tell me. Is it Reg? What's he done now?'

Doreen immediately burst into tears. Daphne sprang at once to her side, producing a hankie from a pocket, and giving her old friend a bearlike hug. 'Oh, whatever is the matter, you poor old sausage?'

The warmth of Daphne's body cheered her up a bit. There was something comforting and motherly about her, and Doreen often thought she would make a great mum. She gazed up into Daphne's big cow eyes and welcoming smile, managing a weak one of her own in response. 'I'm so sorry, Daf, I feel so silly.'

'Come on, dear, tell Auntie Daffers what's wrong. You'll feel better.'

Doreen pulled away from the embrace and blew her nose. 'Well, alright then. You know the other day, Reg went to the cricket, whatever it was, when we won the embers, or whatever it's called.'

'Ashes, dear. Great, wasn't it, England beating Australia. First time since God was a boy! Go on.'

'Yes well, whatever. Well, he didn't get home until seven o'clock. The first thing he did when he got through the door...' Doreen began sniffing again as her friend anticipated another breakdown. 'Oh, Daphne!'

'What?'

'He came straight up to me and... and... kissed me, you know, right on the mouth. He smelled of drink.'

'Well, what's so awful about *that*?' said Daphne, her eyes wide in amazement. 'You are man and wife, aren't you?'

Doreen almost burst into tears again, just about regaining some composure. 'Well, it's just that he's never done that sort of thing before, not even a peck on the cheek. He kept on saying, ''We've done it! We've done it!" repeatedly, and punching his palm with his fist. Honestly, Daphne, I was so embarrassed.'

'What on earth for? He was happy, that's all.'

'Anyway, then he refused his dinner, which I'd made specially. You know, shepherd's pie, his favourite, although sometimes he likes rabbit stew on occasion.'

'Oh Doreen, stop waffling and get to the crux.'

'Sorry. Well, then, like I said, he didn't want his food. Then he announces he's off to his den, to refight the battle of Waterloo, and I didn't see him again until bedtime. I'm lying in bed, you know, reading, and then… and then…' Doreen burst into a flood of tears again, huge sobs emanating from her heaving little body.

'And then, what?'

Doreen looked up into her dear friend's eyes, her own glistening with distress. 'He got into bed with me!' The confession had such an effect on her that she buried her head in Daphne's ample bosom, let out a loud moan, and began sobbing uncontrollably.

'Well, what's so awful about that? You are married, aren't you?' Daphne was doing her best not to burst out laughing.

Doreen lifted her head briefly and blew her nose. 'But he never does that. Never. We've always had single beds, and he's never been interested in, you know, that side of things. And to be honest, I'm not sorry. I've never gone much on it myself.'

'So, then what happened?' asked Daphne, desperately trying to keep a straight face. 'No, don't tell me, let me guess?'

Doreen let go another loud and prolonged moan. 'He never said a word. Not a word. Never even took his pyjamas off. When he finished, he passed wind, got back into his own bed, and was snoring away within a minute or two. Oh Daphne, it's not funny.'

'Yes, I can see how upsetting it must have been for you. Men can be such beasts sometimes, so unfeeling. Perhaps I should have a word with him about it.'

'Oh no, Daphne, please don't. I don't want any trouble.'

'Don't be such a mouse, Doreen. In all seriousness, just because you are man and wife doesn't give him the right to behave like that. You know, he should be reported for that kind of behaviour. Honestly, men! I don't know if I've ever told you about my experiences with them.'

Only about a thousand times, thought Doreen.

'I remember the first time,' Daphne reminisced. 'We must have been about 17; that summer dance in Tumbledon, someone's party or other, remember? It was the first time I'd ever drunk gin, and I got a bit blotto. It's always been my downfall, come to think of it. I was dancing with that spotty lad from school who worked at the garage – Tom Dancy, I think his name was. Anyway, he dragged me outside on the pretext of some "slap and tickle", as he called it. He was a big bloke, and I was well gone. Before I knew what was happening, he had me up against a wall, pulled my draws down, and was, well, like a rat up a drainpipe! All I remember was having a hot flush and being sick afterwards. I had hell to pay when I got home and had to explain the stains in my knickers!'

Doreen blushed and looked awkward. 'Oh Daphne, I wish you wouldn't talk so brazenly about things like that. It's not nice.'

'Oh, don't be such an old prude.' Daphne was warming to her theme. 'Well, that was the first time,' she sighed. 'Then, when I was in the WRENS during the war. I joined up to see the world, to see some action. I could tell you some stories! The only action we saw was under the blankets! Just glorified office girls, we were. Typists. The one time I saw the sea was when they posted us to Plymouth. All us girls were in a bar somewhere, and I had a few too many gins again and got chatted up by this merchant seaman who worked in the engine-room of some old tub or another; stank of oil and grease. Well, bugger me if we didn't end up in some seedy hotel, with him dribbling and slobbering all over me and stoking my boiler all night!'

'Oh honestly, Daphne!'

'It made me feel sick, and I had a sore fanny for a week!'

'Daphne, please don't tell me about things like this. You really are the limit sometimes.'

Daphne giggled at the thought. 'Well, it put me off men for the duration, excuse me, thank you very much. They're all animals, if you want to know. Only after one thing, mucky business!'

'Yes, well…'

'I was in the WRENS, dear. You don't call a spade a shovel there. I'll tell you one thing. I'm glad I never got married. It's all vastly overrated, if you ask me.'

Doreen, feeling more embarrassed, went very quiet, then had a thought. 'But you like Mr. Winford-Harvey, don't you?'

Daphne smiled. 'Yes, well, he's a gentleman, though. That's different.'

'Let's forget all this and have another drink.'

'Good idea.' Daphne gazed at her pal, then asked, 'Did he hurt you?'

'Who?'

'Reg, of course, you daft brush. Who did you think I meant, the milkman?'

'Yes, he did.' Doreen looked on the verge of tears again. 'You know, I don't really love him. I don't think I ever did.'

'Why did you marry him then?'

'I don't know.' Doreen looked down at the carpet. There was a new wine stain there. 'It just seemed the right thing at the time. I was bored with my life, I suppose. He's not a bad old stick, really. He's so clever, and I'm so dull.'

'He's a clot, Dor.'

'No, he's not a clot. He's a very intelligent man. You know what he did in the war, all that top secret stuff? He never talks about it, but he must have saved thousands of lives. People forget that, because he wasn't a fighting soldier.' There was another silence before Doreen asked, 'Did *he* hurt you?'

'Did who hurt me?'

'That smelly seaman in Plymouth?'

'I told you, I had a sore fanny for a week!'

Both women burst out laughing, and hugged each other, then Doreen started snivelling again. 'Oh Daphne, I'm so unhappy. Look at us, we're nearly 40 and what have we got to show for it?'

'Never mind, Dor, we've still got each other.'

'I love you, Daf.'

'I love you, too. Perhaps you should divorce Reg and marry me!'

'Oh Daphne, what on earth are you saying!' Both women, fuelled by the wine, started giggling again.

After a while, the two of them recovered their decorum and began to discuss the big cricket match at the weekend against Rotting Hill. Never mind England v Australia; that paled in comparison to West Rotting versus Rotting Hill!

It was Doreen's sworn duty to make the teas for the cricketers, umpires, and scorers. Daphne was the team scorer, bringing all the neatness and precision of her office duties to bear on the club's leather-bound scorebook, completed after every game to perfection. She always took with her a large case of coloured pencils, rubbers, and pencil sharpeners. Each of the West Rotting team members had their own colour-coded pencil, with which she recorded their batting scores, bowling analyses, catches, run outs, or stumpings, in the appropriate section of the book, along with their ongoing culminative aggregate totals, recorded later at the back of the book every Monday after a game. Daphne's favourite colour was orange, and that was the one allocated to her employer and club captain, Cedric Ashley Winford-Harvey.

Daphne might claim to have an aversion to the male gender in general, but Cedric (as she liked to call him – though never to his face) was the one real love of her life. Sadly, such love was unrequited, as Cedric was married and so engrossed most of the time in not only his business, but also his lifelong passion for cricket, that he scarcely appeared to notice her.

Cedric, popularly known as 'The Commodore', following his wartime career in the navy, had originally employed Daphne as a typist on her demob in 1946. But she had proved so efficient that less than a year later she had become his personal secretary. She proved to be super-efficient. In fact, it was not long before she knew the business inside out. Her filing system was meticulous; on her desk, every pin, paper clip, and pencil in its place, her typewriter always spotless, everything in the office indexed and cross-referenced to perfection.

As the years went by, Cedric had come to rely on her more and more, and in an age of austerity, when sports equipment was something of a luxury, thanks almost entirely due to Daphne, the business had begun to make a decent profit.

He had lost a leg in the war, during an unspecified action in the Far East, though this hadn't prevented him from carrying on playing cricket. He had captained the team since before the war, when he had been an excellent all-round player, and whilst at school had trials for both Sussex and Surrey, though nothing had come of them. He failed to see why the loss of a limb should prevent him from carrying on with the game in the same way. He was also particularly well off, the club's continued existence being almost entirely due to his ongoing benevolence.

Cedric had married Phyllis Aubisson in 1935, from the wealthy Aubisson family of wine merchants. She was also extremely wealthy, and they lived in grand style in a huge pile just outside Beach Cross, a few miles north of

West Rotting. The Winford-Harvey family had been living in India when Cedric was born, though they had returned to England at the outbreak of war in 1914. Cedric had a fine education at Eton and Cambridge, gaining both academic and sporting distinction. In his youth and early manhood, he was an extremely vigorous and virile man, which was just as well for Phyllis, who had the reputation of being a screaming nymphomaniac! The very fact that he alone (most of the time) had been able to satisfy her needs for so many years said a great deal for his libido.

Sadly, on losing his leg, he also lost something else. Though he returned from the war with his tackle undamaged, the emotional scar of his amputation had rendered him impotent, whereupon Phyllis embarked on a series of scandalous affairs with any man within a 50-mile radius. Cedric accepted the inevitability of this and turned a blind eye, so long as she kept up the pretence of being lady of the manor. Once an intemperate and emotional man, he had mellowed since returning from abroad. One thing, however, was guaranteed to raise his blood pressure, and that was cricket, West Rotting cricket in particular; the game having become more of a passion to him than ever. The weekend's fixture against Rotting Hill – his bitter rivals – had occupied his mind for weeks beforehand.

In the office, he would hobble around on his prosthetic limb, puffing fiercely on his pipe whilst dictating to Daphne sitting sedately in her chair. She would pretend to take notes in shorthand, before ignoring everything he had said and composing all the business correspondence herself, which she later presented to her boss for signature. He always duly signed without reading. He knew that her business acumen was greater than his, and she knew that he knew, though each day they would repeat the same charade, both parties comfortable with the status quo. Cedric pretended that he ran the business efficiently, and pretended not to know that it was really Daphne who ran the business so efficiently. As for her feelings, she loved and admired him, but had no ambition at his expense.

She hated that his bitch of a wife was putting it about the whole county – three counties, in fact – and that Cedric did not know or simply no longer cared. The two women detested the sight of one another, though for the sake of professionalism and cordiality, Daphne was forced to be polite to Phyllis on the rare occasions she telephoned or visited the office.

Phyllis's latest affair was with Jimmy Catt, dashing young war hero and presently sales manager at Commodore Sports. He claimed to have fought in the Battle of Britain, though Daphne had sussed out he was a phoney, since she had seen his personnel record and ascertained he was still in short trousers in 1940. Nevertheless, she had to keep her counsel, for Cedric's sake, since he was immensely fond of the lad and had given him a job when he was on his uppers and almost unemployable.

Jimmy was also a prominent member of the West Rotting cricket team and had recently been made vice-captain. The fact that he was now having it away with

Mrs. Winford-Harvey, with everyone appearing to know about it except her husband – or perhaps he knew but no longer cared – made Daphne even more angry and bitter. Fate had dealt poor Cedric such a bad card, and she often wondered how much he was really suffering, though he always presented a brave face. It was almost more than her poor heart could bear.

'How many sandwiches do you think we'll need?' asked Doreen, perking up a bit.

'Oh, I don't know,' replied Daphne. 'Quite a lot, I should think, but plenty of variety.'

'I read in the paper that we'll be having proper bread soon,' pointed out Doreen, referring to the end of food rationing.

'That'll be nice, Dor. Shall I bake a cake? That always goes down well on these occasions.' Daphne seemed to drift away again, thinking of her unrequited love.

'You know, Daf, you've got such nice hair, so thick and shiny. I wish mine was like that. I can't do anything with it. It always looks such a mess, so drab. No wonder Reg never notices me.'

'Oh Doreen, stop feeling sorry for yourself, for goodness' sake! Now look here, girl, you've got to brisk up.' Daphne applied her best hectoring tone, which Doreen found quite intimidating. 'What I think we need is a trip to Tumbledon. First, we'll visit the hairdressers, and then get you some nice new clothes. Perhaps even

Reg might notice you then. Let's go Saturday. What do you think, hmm?'

'I really don't feel up to it,' whined Doreen. 'To be honest, I haven't really felt that well since we went to the Coronation, sitting outside all night in the cold and wet.'

'Yes, I know, but it was worth it just to see the new queen.'

'I'd love to go, but I don't have that much money. Reg gives me hardly anything; just enough for his food. He spends it all on those silly toy soldiers. Anyway, we must get the teas for Sunday.'

'We can do that at the same time,' Daphne pointed out. 'Then we'll get everything ready on Saturday night, so there's no rush on Sunday then. How about that?'

'Oh, alright then. I suppose that'll be alright.'

'Yes, it will,' confirmed Daphne, 'and don't worry about Reg. I'll sort him out. You must get out more, Doreen. All you ever do is potter round that little garden. It's not good for you.'

Unknown to Doreen, Cedric, or anyone else, come to that, Daphne had long been living something of a secret life. Despite her outwardly sunny and cheerful demeanour, she was subject to fits of severe melancholia, particularly on Friday nights after she had finished work for the week. After secretly purchasing a bottle of gin and a packet of cigarettes, she would retire to her solitary existence in her little cottage and indulge herself of an evening in front of her new television, watching some romantic melodrama.

These drunken spasms would spark sexual fantasies as she lay in bed, all involving Cedric; the favourite being the one from the old silent movies where some dastardly villain (always foreign) captured her and tied her to a railway track. Cedric would then gallop to her rescue just in the nick of time to avoid the oncoming train. They would then ride off together into the sunset.

Most of Daphne's fantasies involved her being roughly tied up by some brutish scoundrel, then gallantly saved by Cedric (with a full set of limbs), when she would smother him with kisses, followed by a bout of red hot, rampant, and uninhibited sex. Inevitably, she would wake up in a cold sweat and with a fearful hangover, though usually recover in time for her Sunday cricket duties and work again on the Monday.

Chapter Five

August 22nd

WALLY

Walter Richardson rose late on Saturday morning, as was his habit now to do. And since the death of his wife, he had very much become a creature of habit. The procedure was in direct contrast to weekdays, when he punctually got up on the dot of six o'clock and, after a meagre breakfast, cycled the four miles into Tumbledon, where he worked as a librarian and archivist.

Sitting up, he pushed Barney the collie off his bed. The dog let out an irritated grunt and flopped onto the floor. Each night, the pair would go through the same routine: at bedtime, the dog would dutifully curl up in his basket by the fire in the front room, but when morning came, he would always be found snuggled up on Wally's bed. During the week, Barney would be let out whilst his master was at work, and allowed to roam about the village, meeting up with some of the other dogs, and rummaging for scraps from his human acquaintances.

Wally dressed himself in old shirt and loose trousers, then stumbled into the kitchen to find Barney sitting in his usual position by the door, ready to perform his early morning ablutions. Still half asleep, Wally failed to notice him, and the dog let out a high-pitched yip. His master grunted an apology and unlocked the back door.

The weather was overcast, and it was drizzling gently. Making himself his usual breakfast – cereal, toast, and a cup of tea – Wally sat down at the table and switched on the wireless. After a couple of minutes, Barney returned looking a trifle damp, shook himself, and sat down at Wally's feet to await his own breakfast, usually consisting of the odd scrap of toast and some tea grouts. Wally then pottered about the place for a while, doing nothing in particular – a legacy of days as a prisoner-of-war. Presently, he spotted Barney sitting by the door once more, anticipating his early morning walk.

By way of a change, the pair took the narrow path that led to Barker's farm, on the upwards slope from the village to the top of Rotting Hill. After they had gone a hundred yards or so, a huge black and white Old English Sheepdog appeared, sidled up to Barney, and began sniffing his bottom. Barney had long since lost any interest in such doggie matters, and ignored him. Wally recognised the animal as Henry, the Fishers' pet from The Black Pig.

It was no longer raining, but a fresh breeze had sprung up, cooling the early morning air. In a moment, Hazel came trudging around the bend in the lane. She looked totally different from the rather dishevelled barmaid of the night before, when she had clearly not been at her best. Gone was the barmaid's apron and the cleavage reserved for the patrons; instead, she looked most presentable, in a crisp white blouse and a plain grey skirt.

'Oh, there you are, yer silly mutt. Thought you'd seen a rabbit.'

'No rabbits round here any more,' said Wally. When he saw Hazel, Barney abandoned his sniffing and ran to greet her, tail wagging furiously.

He had not considered much about other women since his wife died, but the sight of the winsome barmaid caused his heart to flutter slightly, which disturbed him. He had always had a soft spot for her, being Janice's best friend in the village. And despite her shady past and occasionally contentious disposition, he had always quite fancied her in a friendly sort of way.

'Looks like rain,' offered Wally, for something to say.

'Weather ok for tomorro', though,' returned Hazel.

'Yes, big game, you coming?'

'You betcha!' she said with enthusiasm. 'Wouldn't miss it f' anything. It's about time we put one over on them snooty buggers, 'specially that Daphne whatsername. Prissy cow, she is. Thinks she's the bleedin' cat's whiskers, that one does!'

Wally smiled to himself. Despite living in the countryside for so many years, Hazel had never lost her Cockney twang, which was especially noticeable when she got excited or raised her voice. They ambled on together for a while, the dogs sniffing everything and following on behind.

'Comin' t' church tomorro'?" asked Hazel out of the blue.

Wally was somewhat taken aback. 'Er... I dunno, haven't been since...'

'Since the funeral?'

'No.'

'Look, Wol, you can tell me to mind me own business if yer like, but it's been a 'ole year now. Yer shouldn't be couped up, rattlin' round that 'ouse with just that soppy dog. It's not 'ealthy. Yer still a young man. All y'ever do is go the cricket or come down the pub now and then.'

Wally looked down at the ground. 'I miss her, Hazel.'

She put her arm inside his as they walked on. 'I miss 'er, too, Wol. She was me best mate. Kept me on the straight an' narrer – most o' th' time, anyway. We 'ad some laughs together, me an' 'er. I 'specially miss 'er at the whist drives we used to go to. We used to win nearly every time. She were good at that sort o' thing, numbers and such; 'ad a good memory f' things like that – clever ol' stick. Then there was that night we won ten quid on the 'ousey 'ousey. We 'ad a few drinks that night!'

'We never did have much time together,' mused Wally, 'what with me being away for so long, stuck in that POW camp. Sometimes, it was only the thought of seeing her again kept me going.'

Hazel's touch felt good to him. Despite her reputation as a bit of a battle-axe, he felt comfortable in her company. There was something comforting and maternal about her. They walked a little slower down the track as the pub came into sight.

'I think I might come to church in the morning, to pray for a victory, if you like,' he suggested. She laughed at the thought. 'What I don't understand is why you go. You don't strike me as being a religious person.'

She laughed again and squeezed his arm. 'Oh Wol, if yer only knew. I only went 'cause Jan used to' go, plus I fancied the vicar.' Wally shot her a puzzled glance. 'Wicked innit?' she giggled like a silly girl. 'I can't 'elp it. I think e's gorgeous, an' the way 'e delivers them sermons makes me go all funny where it shouldn't!' She laughed loudly this time. 'Oh Wol, what am I like?' She almost slipped on the wet grass and grabbed his arm tighter. 'Oops! It ain't just that. I love all the singin', too, all them 'yms. Lovely tunes, some o' them 'yms. Loved singin' at school, 'bout the only thing I were good at. I were always in the choir. We went singin' in Westminster Cathedral once. Dad was the same, always singin' in the bath or the air raid shelters, but he don't go now, not since Mum died.'

By this time, they had reached the back garden gate of the pub, and she slipped the lock so Henry could run inside. She let go of Wally's arm, and he felt somewhat disappointed.

'Well, better go. Got some pies to do. Come round an' 'ave one lunchtime.'

'Hazel, there's something I need to say to you.'

'Oh?'

'When Jan died, and you came round to help me a bit, I felt I pushed you away. I shouldn't have done that. I'm sorry.'

'Oh Wol, don't worry 'bout it. We all 'ave our own way of grieving. It's all water under th' bridge anyway.'

'I'm sorry. It wasn't right. I know you meant well.'

She looked deeply into his sad eyes. 'I promised 'er I'd look out for yer, an' I always will. If y'like, I can come over one day an' cook you a nice dinner, if that's alright.'

'Yes, that would be nice.'

'In the meantime, come round an' 'ave a pie lunchtime.'

'I'll try and get some of the lads to come to church tomorrow.'

'To pray for a victory, eh? Can't do any 'arm, can it?'

For a moment, they both stood there awkwardly, not knowing what to say next, but neither wanting to leave the other. 'Well, I better be gettin' on,' she said. 'Lunch to do.' Barney sat looking up at his master, wondering why they were still standing there.

'OK then, see you lunchtime for my pie.'

'I'll save one for yer.'

'Hazel?'

She had turned to go but stopped. 'What, luv?'

'Oh, it doesn't matter. I'll see you later.'

Wally and Barney strolled around the path that led by the side of the inn until they reached the main road. His mind, for some reason he could not explain, was in a turmoil, thinking of Hazel. He spent the next couple of hours pottering about in his little garden, mowing the small square of lawn, and digging up a few weeds and carrying waste to the heap at the bottom of the garden. Hazel was right; he needed something more to occupy himself. For some reason, he could not get her out of his mind.

At one-thirty, he assiduously locked his door again and trudged back down the hill, with Barney following closely, to The Black Pig. The sky had cleared, and it felt warmer. The sunshine made the old village look brighter, the grass on the green seeming greener, and the windows of the old houses sparkled in the sunshine. Even the old inn was looking its best, with its newly-painted mock Tudor black and white front – one of Billy's little jobs.

Ken Kippax and Alf Fortune were sitting outside on their usual bench, pints of ale half empty. Wally greeted them both then went inside, feeling nervous. Hazel was not in evidence; Bert serving at the bar. 'Hello, Wally. Usual, is it?'

'Three pints, please. Hazel said you had some steak pies in.'

'That's right,' grunted Bert, as he pulled the tap handle back. 'She's in the kitchen doin' 'em now. I'll bring one out when they're ready.'

'Yeah, thanks,' said Wally, straining across Bert to see into the kitchen behind the bar, but there was no sign of Hazel. Bert gave him a tray to carry the drinks out.

'As I was sayin' – thanks, Wol – it's all very well livin' in a home-owning democracy, but most working-class folk can't afford to buy their own places.' Ken was pontificating again about the Conservative government, though much of it was lost on Alf, who knew little about politics and cared even less. 'Six years of Labour,' Ken continued, 'then the bloody Tories come back in an' change everything back again; nationalise, denationalise; people don't know whether they're coming or going. Land fit for heroes, that's a laugh!'

Wally sat down next to Ken, who paused briefly from his tirade to light a cigarette. 'Thought you'd be working today?' Ken was a signalman on the railways.

'Late shift.'

'Surprised you got time for any work, all them union meetings,' offered Alf.

'Least I got a proper job,' responded his drinking pal. 'Least I ain't pissed all my money down the drain.'

'Gravediggin's a proper job,' Alf said, scratching his ruddy, bewhiskered face. 'Someone's gotta do it. Anyway, I 'ad some bad luck with my investments.'

'Yeah, some of 'em are still runnin',' laughed Ken, referencing Alf's misfortunes on the horses. 'Trouble with gravedigging, Alf, there ain't a lot of need for it round 'ere. People don't die that often. There's only 'bout a hundred souls in the village.'

'New graves are always needed,' Alf pointed out.

Upset at the direction the conversation was taking, Wally moved to change the subject. 'Got a team for tomorrow yet?'

The old man pulled the grubby notebook out of his pocket. His hands were dirty, and Wally couldn't help noticing how black and broken his fingernails were.

'Still got a bit of a problem,' advised Alf, scratching his head. 'No-one's seen Charlie. Don't know if he's playin' or not.'

'It's alright, mate,' confirmed Ken. 'Ted spoke to Her Ladyship this morning. Tarquin's definitely coming down for the weekend, bringing some of 'is posh London chums, shouldn't wonder. Right bunch of Hooray Henries, by the sound of it. Tark won't play unless Charlie does, so we should be ok. Ted said Charlie's been away workin' on some garden in Wychurst, but he should be back tonight.'

'That still leaves us one short,' Alf grimaced, scratching his head violently and furrowing his brow. Opening his notebook, he read out a list of names, as follows: 'Charlie, meself, the vic, Tark, Tim, Wally, Barry, Billy, Ken, Ted, and A.N. Other.'

'Who the fuck is "A.N. Other"?' moaned Ken. 'I don't believe this. Most important bleedin' game of the year an' we're struggling for 11!'

'Lots o' folks on 'oliday,' Alf pointed out.

Ken sighed in exasperation. 'There must be 50 able-bodied men in the village. I suppose I could get my boy Ivan to play.'

'How old is he now?' asked Wally.

'Thirteen,' confirmed Ken, 'but 'e's played at school. Still, I don't like the thought of 'im 'avin' to face that Mellors boy.' Michael Mellors, whose family lived in West Rotting, was a young fast bowler currently studying at Sussex University.

'Not playin', is 'e?' said Alf dejectedly. 'Nearly took my bleedin' 'ead off last time! He must be faster than Freddie Trueman!'

'Yeah, not as good, though, otherwise 'e'd be playing for England,' observed Ken, rather stating the obvious. 'It's the summer 'olidays. I 'eard both 'im and Tim Stewart are turning out for Tumbledon this afternoon.'

'That still leaves us one short,' Wally pointed out.

'What about Bert?' suggested Alf, just as the landlord appeared with Wally's hot pie.

'What about Bert what?' queried Bert, handing Wally his pie on a plate.

'Fancy playin' tomorro'?' asked Alf optimistically.

'What, with my bad back? Do me a favour. Don't mind a bit of umpiring, but don't ask me to play.' As if emphasise the point, Bert stood upright stiffly, as if in some discomfort. He had a chubby face, like his daughter, but his worn features marked him out as a man not fit for a game of cricket

'What about Tark's friends?' Wally advocated.

'Oh, stroll on!' declared Ken. 'Bunch of toffee-nosed, chinless wonders. Probably wouldn't know one end of a bat from the other!'

'Could always ask.'

'Well, what are we gonna do then?' Alf was looking more and more perplexed.

'Don't worry, mate, we'll think of something. Another pint then?' Ken suggested.

'I haven't seen Billy today,' said Wally, changing the subject.

'I 'eard 'e was over at the widow Webb's again, putting some shelves up,' Ken said, standing up and stretching.

'He's been doing that for the last couple of weeks,' stated Wally. 'I haven't heard much banging, though.'

'Not on the outside, any road,' laughed Alf. ''E's a sly old devil. Been getting 'is dinner there, so I 'eard.'

'Anything rather than pay for somethin',' opined Ken. 'Been getting more than 'is dinner there, if you ask me.'

They all laughed, and Ken popped inside to get another pint. Wally then remembered the conversation with Hazel. 'Listen, how about getting all the team to go to church in the morning, before the game? It'll be a good starting point for the day.'

'You must be jokin',' said Alf, violently rubbing his nose. 'You wouldn't catch Ken dead in that place. Come t' think of it, that's the only time you would find 'im there!' Alf laughed at his own joke, though Wally was not amused.

'No, I'm serious. I think we should all make an effort, like the vic said. It's only one time. What harm can it do?'

'I'll ask around,' agreed Alf, 'but don't 'old yer breath, like. I ain't never seen any of our lads inside a church, 'cept fer weddings and funerals.'

'Anyway, let's meet up here in the morning,' suggested Wally, getting stuck into his pie. 'Hmm, this is nice. Hazel certainly knows how to cook stuff.' Ken emerged with a pie in one hand and a pint in the other.

'Wally says we're all going to morning service tomorro' to pray for a win,' chortled Alf. 'Pray to the Almighty for a win over the Rotters.'

'Huh! Gonna need more than that,' scoffed Ken, balancing a pint, a cigarette, and the pie between his two hands.

'You know, Wol, it ain't such a daft idea,' Alf said. 'The missus is always moaning at me to go. I might get in 'er good books for a spell.'

'Well, count me out,' mumbled Ken, through a mouthful of pie.

'Ah, you be a godless creature, an' no mistake,' said Alf.

'Too right, mate, but at least I ain't a hypocrite. Don't believe in any of it, an' that's flat.'

Time passed with the old friends, and shortly the church clock struck three, as Alf and Ken drank up and went off to their work. Wally and Barney hung around for a bit, hoping that Hazel might appear to clear the glasses. When she didn't show, he took them inside himself, but only Bert was at the bar. He waved a farewell and off they wandered.

'Come on, Barney, got to buy something for dinner.'

Chapter Six

August 22nd

KEN

Saturday night at The Black Pig was always something
of a clamorous affair, as most of the village would be
there, mainly because there was little else to do socially,
unless one went to the nearest cinema or dancehall, four
miles away in Tumbledon.

It was a fine, warm evening, and the benches outside the
inn were soon occupied. Extra bar staff were called in
for Saturdays, one of whom was Farmer Barker's
daughter, Emily, on holiday from college in London.
It was rumoured young Tim Stewart, something of a
local Lothario, had been sniffing around her, which was
one of the reasons why he had been barred. However, in
the interests of team spirit, Bert Fisher had lifted the ban
following a plea from Ken.

Ken Kippax, Ted Jolly, and Alf Fortune were drinking
outside, when at eight o'clock, a noisy red sports car
drew up outside and Tarquin St. Charles emerged,
accompanied by two young women, both giggling
furiously. He was a tall man, like his elder brother, with

thick, blond hair and a moustache to match. The two girls – one dressed in pink, the other in red – looked somewhat out of place in a country pub.

'Hello, chaps!' greeted Tarquin, in his typically hearty manner.

Ted thought he was an over-privileged pompous twerp, but Ken liked him. Alf liked him, too, and responded with, 'Pleased to see yer. I 'ope you'll be playin' tomorro'.'

'Absolutely, old boy. I should jolly well say so. Social highlight of the year in these parts. Brought a couple of popsies down from London for the weekend to brighten up the old place.' He introduced the shorter of the two girls – the one in the pink dress, who had short brown hair and too much red lipstick. 'This is Fiona...' Then, putting an arm around the other woman, he added, '...and this is Caroline.'

Caroline pouted and looked bored. She was tall and blonde, with a thin, severe face, adorned with piles of curls on the top of her head, the rest of her hair long and straight.

'Pleased t' meet yer,' beamed Alf, offering his hand.

Fiona shook it limply, then giggled. 'Tark thinks I look like Elizabeth Taylor.'

'Oh no,' flirted Alf, still fancying himself as something of a ladies' man. 'You're much prettier than 'er. Can I get you ladies a drink?'

'That's terribly sweet of you,' gushed Fiona. 'Did you hear that, Tark?'

'Do me a favour, Alf,' said Ken wearily, catching the exchange, as the old man escorted the popsies inside.

'What a quaint little place,' said the haughty Caroline as she wiggled off. 'Terribly oldie worldy.'

'Toffee-nosed tarts!' sneered Ted, once the girls had disappeared inside.

'Actually, they're from very good families,' Tarquin pointed out. 'They've both just come out this year.'

'Come out of what, a knocking-shop?' mocked Ted.

'The trouble with you is, you just don't like women,' scoffed Barry Dick, who had suddenly appeared out of nowhere.

'What do you mean by that?' Ted bristled.

'You know what I mean,' scoffed Barry, wandering off into the pub.

'Seen your brother?' Ken enquired of Tarquin, offering him a cigarette.

'Coming over later, I believe. Gone to see Mama. Look, chaps, don't wish to appear rude, but I'd better keep a jolly old eye on the popsies. Not used to these kinds of places; socially, I mean. Don't want them dropping a clanger.'

*

At precisely eight-thirty, the telephone rang in the Barclay household, which was particularly irritating as Doreen and Daphne were listening to an exciting weekly drama serial on the wireless. Doreen cursed and rushed out into the hallway to answer it.

'Tumbledon 237.'

'Oh, hello, old girl, how's tricks?' Doreen instantly recognized the voice at the other end as Cedric Winford-Harvey. 'Cedric here. Bright-eyed and bushy-tailed, I hope?'

'Not too bad, I suppose,' answered Doreen dreamily.

'Reg about?'

'I think he's upstairs playing with his soldiers,' she sighed. 'The last I heard, the Light Brigade were about to charge.'

'All set for tomorrow?'

'Spread fit for a king. Daphne's been here helping me organise it all.'

'You're such a brick, Doreen. Daffers, too. Don't know what we would do without you both. Reg about? Quick word?'

'Just a minute.'

Reg, somewhat perturbed at being disturbed mid-battle, grumbled at Doreen and lurched his way down the stairs to pick up the phone.

'Skip?'

'Reg, old boy, how are you?' The Commodore was brim-full of bonhomie, as per usual.

'Just fighting the battle of Balaclava, actually.'

'Splendid, old son. Winning, are we? All shipshape for tomorrow?'

'Can't wait for it.'

'Action stations, old chap. Action stations. Got the team sorted out. Fit to play, I hope? Percy's dropped out. Bit of a cock-up on the mother-in-law front, apparently. Dinner party. Long-standing engagement. Frightful bore. Need you to plug the gap.' Cedric had a habit of speaking in short sentences, which irritated Reg, though Daphne found it rather endearing. 'I understand Daphne's there. Quick word.'

Reg felt a trifle peeved, since he presumed he'd been selected in the first place. 'Wants to speak to you.' He brusquely handed the phone to Daphne and stormed off.

'Daphne Charters here.'

'Daffers, old girl, no need to be so formal. Not at work now.'

'Sorry, Mister Winford-Harvey.'

'Now look here, Daffers, you silly goose, you can call me Cedric outside the office.'

'If you don't mind,' purred Daphne, crossing her legs and unaware she had a silly grin all over her face.

'Not really, old thing. Just to say hello. Always nice to speak to you.'

Warmed and emboldened by some of Reg's home-made wine, her heart began to beat faster. 'Well, it's always nice to speak to you… Cedric,' Daphne emphasised each succeeding word more strongly. Cedric coughed nervously at the other end of the phone as she added, 'You know, Cedric, you can always ring me at home, any time.'

Cedric coughed again. 'Ahem, yes well, er… must dash. Taking Phyllis to a dinner party. Posh do, what? Old navy chum. Catch up Sunday.'

Daphne slammed the phone down and scowled. 'Bloody woman!' Her mood was temporarily down, but she soon recovered when she thought of poor Cedric.

'You all right, Daf?'

Daphne grinned and licked her lips. 'Oh, he's got such a lovely dark brown voice. It makes my ladybits go all squidgy!'

'Oh Daf, I don't know,' said Doreen. 'You really are the limit sometimes!'

'One day,' murmured Daphne to herself.

*

Meanwhile, back at The Black Pig, the party was just getting started. Young Tim Stewart had arrived, along with Rupert St. Charles. Despite his well-documented social mishaps, Tim was a likeable lad and well educated, but his predilection for the local ale made him a somewhat unpredictable character, both on and off the cricket field.

Charlie, who had a worldly nuance for summing people up in a short phrase, dubbed him 'a ticking popgun'. It wasn't long before Tim had eyed up the two London debs and was trying to engage them in conversation, much to the irritation of Emily Barker, observing them from behind the bar.

Tim was a tallish man, with a thin and wiry frame that belied his strength and athleticism. His hair was cropped short and untidy, but endless days in the fields working for his father had left him tanned, muscular, and not unattractive. Two years of National Service had toughened him up further.

Charlie, on the other hand, looked anything but the heir to a peerage, though that had been in doubt for some while, due to his father's absence and his mother's eccentricity. Not to mention his political views regarding the privileged aristocracy. He wore little more than rags; his trousers were torn at the knees, his shirt grubby, with half its buttons missing, and his light brown hair was lank and hadn't seen a comb or a pair of scissors for months. Yet he had never lost that aristocratic nobility of feature. He was particularly chummy with Ken Kippax, which seemed odd on the surface, though they were both educated men, intellectual in their own ways. They were standing inside by the bar, which was now becoming crowded.

'Looks like we're strugglin' for eleven tomorrow,' moaned Ken, as Charlie cadged a cigarette from him.

'Isn't that ever the case?' Charlie spoke in a slightly scoffing tone, especially when talking to Ken, though the latter pretended never to notice. 'I thought about dropping myself. My form's been so bad this season.' He was mocking his chum in his usual light-hearted manner and smiled when he extracted exactly the response expected.

'No way, mate, we need you. We couldn't beat those bastards without you.'

Charlie beamed broadly. 'Well, it is really heartening to hear you say that.'

'No, it's true,' confirmed Ken. 'Who else could captain the side?'

'Who indeed?' agreed the captain.

Just at that moment, Caroline appeared and spoke to Charlie, looking a trifle flustered. 'I say, Rupert, that yokel over there is trying to chat up Fiona.' She spoke with a clipped, condescending Home Counties accent, pointing to Tim. He was attempting to ignite a cigarette he had rolled for Fiona, which was proving difficult due to her giggling every time he attempted to put a lighted match to it. Eventually, they managed to get it going, only for her to take a deep drag and then cough violently between more giggles.

'Is he alright?' she enquired. 'I think Fi's getting a bit sloshed, ya.'

'He's actually quite a young gentleman,' Charlie explained. 'His father's a local magistrate and owns much of the land around here.'

'Oh, really, ya,' said Caroline, changing her tone and almost breaking into a smile. 'Well, perhaps I'd better go and offer a bit of support then. These old places can be such a hoot, can't they?'

'Know what that one needs. Toffee-nosed bitch!' offered Ken, as she wiggled off.

'What's that then?' Charlie grinned.

'Stiff cock up between 'er legs!' A large pile of ash fell from the cigarette hanging from his mouth.

'Why don't you suggest that to her?' advocated Charlie, still grinning.

'No thanks, mate.' Ken looked a bit flustered himself, as if the conversation was perhaps drifting away from his usual domain. 'Won't catch me hobnobbing with the upper classes.'

'Ken, you're such as snob,' teased Charlie, enjoying the encounter. 'Such a class warrior.'

'Bloody right, mate.' Ken lit another cigarette, feeling a little out on a limb.

Sitting at a table in the corner, Tim was getting on famously with Fiona and Caroline, Tarquin having stepped outside for a breath of fresh air. Having downed a few drinks, Caroline's haughty expression was slowly disappearing as she listened intently to Tim explaining the intricacies of the game of cricket.

'So, do you run lots of times and knock heaps of wickets over?' she asked, her hand now holding Tim's firmly on the table, preventing him lifting his pint glass.

'Oh yeah, plenty of that,' he replied, warming to the flirtation.

'And catch lots of balls?' Fiona looked a trifle giddy and hooted with laughter at her friend's suggestion.

'Lots.'

'I bet you bowl lots of maidens over,' said Fiona, shrieking with laughter so loudly that heads began to turn to see what was happening.

Emily Barker suddenly appeared, picking up some empty glasses, her expression frosty. 'Having fun, are we?'

'Yes, thank you,' quipped Tim, desperately attempting to keep a straight face. Emily snatched up the glasses and breezed off.

'I say, Timbo,' Caroline asked, 'is that one of your local, what do you call them – "bints" – ha, ha, ha, oh ya?' Fiona began to giggle madly.

Caroline leant forward, squeezed Tim's hand harder, and looked him straight in the eyes. 'Tell me, are you playing "doctors and nurses"' with her?' Both girls burst into uncontrolled laughter, and Tim began to feel slightly embarrassed.

'Not at this precise moment,' he replied, not quite understanding what she meant, though he could hazard a good guess.

'I think we need to go outside,' Caroline said. 'We need a spot of air.'

'Good idea,' Tim agreed, and followed them both unsteadily out of the door.

Meanwhile, Billy Moon had arrived and was getting his first drink from the bar, not having attracted anyone else's attention to buy him one. He noticed Hazel was looking a good deal perkier than their previous meeting. He spotted she'd had her hair permed that afternoon and complimented her on it

She gave him an odd look, handing over his pint, and asked,' Seen Wally tonight?'

'Er... no, don't think I have.' She began to move away to serve another customer, only for Billy to stop her. 'Hazel.'

'What is it? I got people to serve.'

"Well, erm... I was wondering, like, erm... if you still, you know, had the painters in, or whether it's alright to have another bunk-up?'

Hazel glared at him in astonishment. 'Stone me, Billy, you really know 'ow t'sweet-talk a girl!'

'Is that a yes, then?' he asked nervously.

'I'll fink about it, but don't 'old yer breaf.'

*

Wally had decided to have a quiet night indoors, not feeling like facing all the hubbub down the pub, and preferring to get a good night's sleep before the big match the next day. He had never been a great drinker or much of a social animal, and only visited the pub occasionally for a spot of company. After his wife's death, he had tended to withdraw inside himself, despite Hazel's efforts. He preferred his own company most of the time, and it wasn't as if he was completely alone, for there always the faithful Barney.

He settled down in his armchair with a book – *Brightly Fades the Don*, by the Australian writer and former Test batsman Jack Fingleton, recounting the last Aussie tour to England in 1948. At ten-thirty, he decided to go to bed, taking the book with him. As he closed it and stood up, he glanced at Janice's photograph on the mantelpiece. Oddly, he was not thinking of her at that moment, but Hazel instead, which puzzled him.

'Basket, Barney,' he absent-mindedly commanded his dog. The collie dutifully crept into his basket and snuggled down, head resting on his paws, though keeping his eyes wide, watching Wally go first into the bathroom, and then the bedroom. He waited until Wally's bedside light went out, then quietly rose and padded through the bedroom door. Satisfied he could hear the familiar sound of Wally snoring, he jumped stealthily on the bed and curled up at his master's feet.

*

Chucking-out time at The Black Pig could be anything between midnight and one in the morning. Despite the prevailing licensing laws, the local policeman – if he ever bothered to patrol Rotting Hill, which was practically never – usually turned a blind eye if there wasn't too much noise.

Whenever the men of the village got together and sunk a few pints, the conversation inevitably got around to their war exploits. Although Europe had been at peace for eight years, it was never far from anyone's mind. Fortunately, the village had not suffered anything like as badly as in 1914-18, when almost every family had lost a loved one.

The war exploits of the cricket team were varied: Ted Jolly had been a 'Bevin Boy', recruited to serve in the Kent coal mines instead of the armed forces, and it proved a stigma he carried around and would rather forget; Wally had volunteered on the outbreak of war, only to find himself cut off at Calais in 1940, following the BEF'S headlong retreat, spending the next five years in a prisoner of war camp; Barry and Charlie, by different means, had managed to avoid a call-up; and Billy spent most of the war loading bombers in England.

Ken, though, was a different story. At one time or another, depending on which tale you believed, he was rumoured to have been a commando, or parachuted behind enemy lines, or perhaps the first man ashore on the Normandy beaches in 1944. How these legends originated was unclear, though Ken neither confirmed nor denied them, which merely added to the legend. One of his mates' great pastimes was ribbing him constantly over his war exploits. At their very mention, he would immediately stiffen, sit up straight, and a serious expression spread across his face.

'How many Germans did you kill then?' he would be teased.

'What's it like killing someone?'

'Night patrols were the worst thing,' Ken would begin. 'You 'ad to creep up behind their sentries and put your 'and over their mouths whilst you slit their throats, stop 'em gurglin'.'

And so it would go on. In reality, Ken had landed on the Normandy beaches, but a week after D-Day, with an engineers' battalion. His famous shrapnel wound, which often began to pain him when his bowling got clattered, was really a dislocated disc in his back, caused by slipping on the ice when he got roaring drunk at Christmas 1944.

His chief protagonist in this ribaldry would invariably be Alf, whose service record exceeded everybody's, though he never boasted of it. He was the only member of the team to have fought in both wars. Conscripted in 1918, he had fired a few shots at the retreating Germans shortly before the armistice, and he re-joined the colours in 1940, only to find himself waist-deep in the sea at Dunkirk, where he had barely escaped with his life.

Hazel called last orders at 12.15, her father having long since retired for the night, and there were still a few customers about. Ken Kippax and Ted Jolly, sinking the remnants of their eighth pint, were still grumbling away to each other and anyone else still prepared to listen. Charlie and Tarquin sat in the corner of the bar, deep in conversation, no doubt discussing some heavyweight topic or other. Tarquin seemed particularly unsteady when he tried to get up from his seat, having long since forgotten about his female companions, last seen on either arm of Tim Stewart, staggering up the hill towards his father's farm.

Billy was leaning on the bar, talking to Hazel, making another feeble attempt to woo her as she polished some glasses.

'Turn it up, Billy,' she said, speaking with a cigarette in her mouth. 'I'm not in the mood, and where were you finkin' of taking me? I don't fink yer ol' mum would be too 'appy if you brought me 'ome in the middle o' the night.'

'You were in the mood a couple of weeks ago,' he said sulkily, a little worse for beer.

Hazel took the cigarette out of her mouth and looked him straight in the eye, noticing Ken and Ted were watching them from the other end of the bar. 'Now, see 'ere, Bill. I've been on me feet all day an' I'm dog tired, so be a good boy an' bugger off!'

'But what about…?'

'What about what?'

'The other day, you know, you and me?'

Hazel sighed, put down the glass she was polishing, and fixed him with an intense glare. 'Look, Billy, there is no you and me. We both got a bit Brahms an' ended up 'avin' a bit o' the other. It shouldn't 'ave 'appened, an' it won't 'appen again, alright? We're friends, ain't we? Let's just keep it that way.' With that, she walked off to the other end of the bar.

Billy looked crestfallen and, glancing up, saw Ken grinning at him. 'Still playin' 'ard to get, is she?' he cackled as Billy joined him and Ted. 'I'd stick to ol' widow Webb if I was you. You're on safer ground there, mate.'

Billy began to hiccup and stumbled towards the door. 'I don't know what you mean… hic… I do little jobs for her, 'cause she's got great… hic… hospital mentality.'

'Got what?' said Ted, pulling a face.

'He means hospitality,' clarified Ken. 'Night, Billy, up early for church.'

'Wassat?' asked Ted, looking mystified.

''Aven't you 'eard? We're all off to church tomorrow, to pray for a win!'

Chapter Seven

August 23rd 8.50am

BILLY

Dawn broke over the valleys of the English Weald, its rolling slopes and dales skirted with a soft haze. The sky was soon cloudless, and as the sun rose crimson in the east, it was clearly going to be a warm day. In Primrose Cottage, the home of Walter Richardson, Barney the black and white collie dog had roused himself, unlike his master, who was still deep in the land of nod.

Wally was dreaming. It was the final Test at the Oval, with the series in the balance at 2-2. On the final day, England needed 200 runs to win the match and The Ashes, but Lindwall and Miller, the Australian fast bowlers, had blasted away the cream of England's batting. Only Denis Compton remained, as Wally joined him at eight wickets down and 80 runs still needed.

'Don't worry, old boy, 'said Denis, greeting him cheerily as Wally shuffled to the wicket amidst the stifling tension. 'Leave it to me. You just keep your end up.'

Easier said than done, thought Wally, as England's cavalier batsman pushed back his thick, black, wavy hair and stood imperturbably at the non-striker's end as Wally somehow blocked out the last two balls of Lindwall's over. Denis then skilfully began to farm the bowling, bisecting the field perfectly to score the odd single to keep the strike, interspersed with the occasional flamboyant stroke to the boundary. Never the best judge of a run, he almost ran Wally out on a couple of occasions, but somehow, he survived.

Slowly, the score mounted as the Aussies began to get rattled. Their captain took the new ball, throwing it to Keith Miller. For once, Denis had failed to pinch the strike, and it was Wally having to face the onslaught. The field closed in as the burly all-rounder lumbered in to bowl off his annoyingly short run-up. The first two balls of the over were short outside the off stump and whistled past Wally's head as he moved away. He could feel the sweat running down his back as the big Aussie steamed in again, off an even shorter run. Wally saw it coming, but froze, unable to move his arms. The red leather projectile hit him square between the eyes and he slumped, poleaxed, on the famous turf.

Still dazed, he felt something sticky and wet on his face. 'Bloody hell, Barney, what are you doing?' he cried, pushing the dog away from licking his face. Barney jumped down on to the floor and began to bark.

Wally glanced at his alarm clock – ten minutes to nine. 'What's the matter with you?' he grumbled, annoyed at being awakened from a long and peaceful slumber.

Barney barked once more, then ran to the door. Wally suddenly realised there was somebody banging on it.

'Oh, gawd, who's that at this time of the morning?' He pulled on his vest and an old pair of breeches and stumbled to the door, opening it to be confronted with the apparition of Billy Moon, dressed in his demob suit, which looked a size too big for him.

'Bloody hell, Billy, what do you want?'

'Sorry to disturb you. Didn't realise you'd still be in bed,' explained Billy, timidly. Barney took the opportunity to scuttle out of the door, immediately cocking his leg on one of the rose bushes in the front garden. 'I was wondering whether you were going to church this morning.'

'What?' mumbled Wally, rubbing the sleep from his eyes.

'Ken said we're all going to church, to pray for a win.'

'I think he must have been pulling your leg, Billy. Anyway, now you're here, you better come in.'

'Any chance of some breakfast?' Billy sat himself down at the kitchen table. His mass of black curls had been unusually combed, rather brutally, and smeared with hair grease, so much so that Wally could smell it. He smiled to himself, remembering Charlie's description of the big man – 'A pig in glasses'.

'Haven't you had any? Your old mum not up yet?'

Billy ignored him as Wally cut a couple of slices of bread from the loaf on the kitchen table.

'Mum don't get up 'til late on a Sunday.'

Wally guessed that Billy's old mum rarely got up at all, and in fact had not been seen in public for some months, amidst local gossip that he had bumped her off and buried her under the floorboards, like the infamous Notting Hill serial killer John Christie, recently hanged for his crimes.

'What's up, Bill, can't you find the church on your own? It's big enough.'

Billy ignored Wally's question and asked for some tea. Wally filled up the battered old kettle at the sink and lit the stove, just then recalling his promise to Hazel about going to church.

'Hazel said we're all off to church today. Morning Service, or something. She said it would be good for morals.'

'Morale,' Wally corrected.

Billy roughly spread some butter on the bread. 'Got any jam?'

Wally wandered over to the kitchen cabinet and pulled down a pot of marmalade. 'Only this.'

'Yeah, that'll do.' Billy dipped a spoon into the pot and emptied a large dollop onto the bread and butter, folded the slice in half, and stuffed it in his mouth. Barney, having emptied his bladder and had a good sniff around the garden, came indoors, sat behind Billy, and yipped loudly.

'What's up with him?'

'He's hungry.'

'You better feed him then. What time's church?'

Wally thought for a minute. 'Dunno, about ten, I think.'

Whilst Billy stuffed his face with bread, marmalade, and anything else edible he could find, slurping down several cups of tea in-between mouthfuls, Wally was busy searching his wardrobe, pondering whether he should put on his best suit for the occasion or the one he wore to work. His best one – a black pinstripe – had last been seen at his wife's funeral, and previous to that at their wedding back in 1937. Seeing it again made him feel heavy-hearted for a moment. Then he pulled it from the rack and dusted it down. He thought of Hazel again; she would like him to wear it.

*

Billy and Wally were far too early, so sat outside the church on the bench by the front entrance. When the Reverend Christian appeared, he was clearly startled at the sight of the pair. 'Good grief, to what do we owe this pleasure?'

The vicar was looking very saintly in his long black and white cassock.

'That's no way to welcome two stray sheep back into the flock,' said Wally, whimsically.

'Hazel's idea,' blurted out Billy. 'Come to pray for victory at the Rotters this afternoon.'

'Ah, I see,' said the vicar, as if the light had suddenly dawned on him. 'Well, you know you are welcome here any time.' He then went inside the church, shaking his head in bewilderment.

'Do you think we should go in?' asked Wally, unsure of the form.

'Better wait 'til everyone else arrives,' suggested Billy. 'We don't wanna sit too near the front.'

Presently, other worshippers began to appear, all giving the two men strange looks as they entered through the large oak door. After a while, Alf Fortune shuffled up, dressed in a grimy-looking grey suit, accompanied by his wife – a grim-faced, tight-lipped woman in a hideous green dress.

'Morning, lads,' he said gaily on passing.

'Morning, Alf, morning, Mrs. F,' Billy chirped. The old woman grunted and passed by.

'I don't think this is such a good idea,' commented Billy. 'Everyone's looking at us.'

Wally didn't reply, as he spotted a plump though comely looking woman in a smart blue and white dress approaching. She wore a straw hat, with a long blue ribbon hanging from it. Her long, curly hair was piled up underneath and pinned neatly at the side. It was only when she was a few yards away that the pair recognised Hazel.

Billy's eyes nearly popped out as she breezed past with a smile. 'Morning, boys.'

'Blimey, she looks almost respectable!' he gasped.

'And why not?' Wally said. 'Come on, let's go in.' They joined the congregation and sat themselves down in a pew about halfway down the aisle, two rows behind Hazel, who was seated next to the Fortunes.

An organ was shimmering somewhere in the distance as Billy glanced around nervously. 'I don't like it 'ere,' he whispered. 'These places give me the wallies.'

'You mean the willies,' corrected Wally. Just then, Hazel glanced round and winked.

'Oi, why's she winking at me?' asked Billy.

She's winking at me, not you, Wally thought to himself, then felt childish for thinking like that.

'Where's the rest of the team? Where's Ken and Ted?' Billy wondered, still glancing about nervously.

'I told you, it's a leg pull,' confirmed Wally. 'Ken won't come. He's an atheist.'

'What's an athist?'

'Someone who doesn't believe in God.'

'I think I'm one of them.' Billy spoke so loudly that a woman in the pew in front, who Wally recognised as Mrs. Durban, the postmistress, turned and shushed him.

'So why are we here then?' Billy whispered as low as he could.

'Because Hazel asked us.' Wally gazed up to look at her. She half-turned, but only to speak to Edith Fortune.

'I want to go to the toilet,' complained Billy. 'Where's the khazi?'

'They don't have khazis in churches. You shouldn't have drunk so many cups of tea. You'll have to tie a knot in it.'

Mrs. Durban turned round again, giving them both another disapproving glare. Hazel must have heard them too, as she turned and pulled a face. Fortunately, at that moment, the Reverend Christian ascended the pulpit.

'Is that the scoreboard over there?' asked Billy, pointing to a board on the wall containing three sets of numbers.

'They're the hymn numbers we're going to sing, you twit! From that hymn book you're holding.' Wally was getting ever more irritated with his companion, as more heads began to turn and glare.

'We shall now sing hymn number 168,' announced the Reverend.

'See, that's the first number,' confirmed Wally, sharing his hymn book with Billy.

The organ piped up and they began singing; at least, Wally mouthed the words, being tone deaf, whilst Billy, completely out of tune, was about half a bar behind everybody else. Up in front, they could hear Hazel's voice booming above all others. It was sweet and clear and made Wally catch his breath; he'd no idea she could sing like that. The rest of the congregation seemed to follow her lead.

When the hymn was finished, Reverend Christian spoke, his imperious voice echoing about the high, wide walls of the church. 'Let us lift up our hearts and give praise to God on this lovely day,' and then, with a puckish grin, 'and let us give praise also for England's great win over Australia.' Wally smiled to himself. Ahead, Alf gave a chuckle, too. 'Let us pray also for a fine game of cricket and a win over West Rotting this afternoon,' the vicar continued, '...and let the match be played in the best spirit and traditions of the noble game.'

More hymns followed, and soon it was all over, and everyone was outside chatting in the sunlight. 'Well,' said Wally, as Mr. and Mrs. Fortune joined him in the garden, 'we're bound to win now, with God's blessing.'

He stood there for a while, hoping Hazel might appear, Billy having hurried away to relieve his bladder. After five minutes, she hadn't appeared, so he went back inside the church, but there was no sign of her, just the doddery old verger collecting up the hymn books from the racks at the back of each pew. Then a thought struck him, and he wandered out again and around the side of the building, along the gravel path to the neatly tended graveyard at the back. There, a woman in a blue and white flowery dress was standing by a gravestone, re-arranging some flowers she had put there only a few days earlier. Wally did not need to know whose grave it was, and for a moment his eyes moistened. Hazel did not see him, but he could hear her talking, though could not make out what she was saying. He walked away before she could see him, embarrassed at being there.

He pondered whether to wait for her at the front again, but decided against it, and began to walk off down the hill to his cottage. Barney, who had been sunning himself on the lawn, jumped up on seeing his master, and lazily padded up to him.

'I hope you haven't left any business here,' he joked. The dog gave him a critical look. 'Come on, then.' But Barney didn't budge as Wally wandered off in a dream, then started barking when his master had gone about

20 yards. 'What's the matter, you silly mutt?' Barney turned his head back towards the church.

'All right, stay there then,' moaned Wally. The dog looked sadly back to the church again, whimpered once, then reluctantly tripped behind Wally.

Wally's mind was whirling again as he packed his whites into his battered old leather cricket bag. He couldn't get Hazel out of his head. Today he had seen a totally different woman, one he had never known: her smart appearance, her lovely singing, the moment at Janice's grave. He stuffed in the dilapidated old cricket bat, held together with yards of tape. It was on its last legs. He kept promising himself to buy a new one, then remembered he had also promised to retire from playing at the end of the summer. It was all getting too much, and he wasn't getting any younger. Anyway, the old bat was special: his wife had bought it for him, and his great hero, Denis Compton, had signed it at a charity match in 1947, though the signature was barely visible now.

He stopped packing the bag for a moment and gazed out of the window, staring at nothing. He turned back, sighing, to find Barney sitting on the bed, watching with those big doggie eyes. 'What are you gawping at, you soppy dog? And get off my bed!'

Chapter Eight

August 23Rd 1.10pm

JIMMY

The clock on Phyllis Winford-Harvey's bedside table read ten minutes past one. Lying on top of her, Jimmy Catt was concentrated with his efforts, but had one eye on the clock. The bed springs were squeaking loudly, and he could hear Phyllis moaning, though more with frustration than pleasure.

'Oh, for God's sake, James, there must be more of you than that! Whatever is wrong with you?'

Jimmy grunted and rolled over. 'Sorry, old girl, engine misfiring. Too much grog lunchtime.' Phyllis sighed and tutted, reaching for her cigarettes on the bedside table.

Jimmy sat up on the side of the bed, looking down. 'No, sorry. Tommy Todger's gone belly-up. Can't understand it. Never happened before.'

'Oh, for Christ's sake, can't you talk proper grown-up English!' complained Phyllis. 'You're not in the RAF now. I'm beginning to wonder if you ever were. Have you seen my lighter?'

'Of course I was in the RAF. Fought in the Battle of Britain. Don't like to talk about it. Lot of good chaps bought it. Bad show.'

Phyllis watched him as he got dressed. He was a handsome man, she had to admit. That was what had attracted her to him in the first place. He stood tall, with a lean and supple body, straight fair hair, and a boyish face masked by a thick moustache. Until today, his athletic lovemaking had excited her endlessly.

'Oh, don't play that reluctant war hero scene. If you fought in the Battle of Britain, you must have done it in short trousers.'

Jimmy ignored her. There were times when she drove him mad. He could have had any woman he wanted, with his genial nature and rakish good looks, but he had lumbered himself with a clapped-out alcoholic nymphomaniac – the wife of his employer and cricket captain – and was feeling increasingly guilty about the affair. That might have had something to do with his recent performance, or rather lack of it, that afternoon.

Phyllis sat up on the bed, folded her arms, and watched him get dressed into his cricket flannels, then his purple and green striped blazer. 'Well, you may as well bugger off and play your stupid cricket,' she smirked, 'seeing as you're not much use here.'

Her words cut right through him; he wasn't used to being spoken to like that. *If I wasn't such a gentleman*, he thought to himself, *I'd give the old bitch a good slap*. She wasn't looking that great herself; not much to look at once the war paint wore off, though she still had a good body for a woman of 45, and knew enough tricks to keep him well satisfied.

'Spoilt bitch!' he muttered, tying a white choker around his neck.

'I heard that,' she hissed. 'My God, you're not even man enough to insult me to my face.'

'Alright then, SPOILT BITCH!' He spat the words at her, angry with himself for being so easily riled. He hardly ever lost his temper.

'That's more like it. I'll make a man of you yet.'

This time, Jimmy did not rise to the bait. In his current condition, he could not rise to anything. 'Are you coming?' he asked evenly, standing rigidly by the bed.

She thought how absurd he looked. 'Obviously you're not. Pity "Tommy Todger" couldn't stand to attention the way you are now.' Jimmy was not amused. 'I suppose I'll have to put in appearance later,' she sighed, throwing off the bedclothes. 'Right now, I'm going to have a bath, so you can run along. And don't make a noise in that jalopy.'

Once outside, Jimmy climbed into his green MG sports car – his pride and joy. He had bought it on the 'never-never', though nobody knew. He was feeling guilty, because Cedric had given him a job at Commodore Sports when he was on his uppers. Cedric had been at Eton with Jimmy's father. Jimmy had gone straight from public school to a commission in the RAF, but that was in 1945, and by the time he had completed his basic training, the show was practically over. With nowhere to go after the war, Cedric had taken him on in his sports firm venture as a favour, after a spot of paternal influence. Jimmy had grown a moustache to make himself look older, and even dyed his hair grey at the temples for effect, so he could pretend he had been one of 'the few'.

Jimmy knew he wasn't all that good at the job, but appearances were everything. His image was good for the company, and it impressed the clients. Cedric knew the truth, and so did Daphne Charters. She ran the show, of course; Cedric knew that and so did Jimmy. He was a bit scared of Daphne and was careful not to upset her in any way – no point in capsizing the applecart or crapping in one's own nest. The old boy was very fond of him and treated him like the son he'd never had; he'd even made him vice-captain of the cricket team. All the chaps called him 'Pussy' like in the forces, and everyone looked up to him. Now he was repaying his benefactor by satisfying his bitch of a wife, or perhaps that was all part of the deal. Did Cedric know? He knew Daphne probably knew. Jimmy knew he was a fraud, but so were a lot of others in West Rotting and their exclusive little cricket club.

He was late for the game. He'd better get a move on. The match was due to start at 2 o'clock, though in reality it rarely did. Cedric would be fretting, as he always did until everyone in the team showed up. Fortunately, being a Sunday, there were no servants around in the Winford-Harvey residence, converted from an old manor house and set in its palatial own grounds.

He clicked the engine into life, violently revving it up to annoy Phyllis. With a mighty roar and the squeal of rubber on gravel, the car screeched off towards the main road. Instantly it made him feel better, his heart racing along with the fast car. Chocks away! Grab the joystick! Bandits at nine o'clock! Tally ho!

Chapter Nine

August 23rd 1.30pm

WEST ROTTING

The Rotting Hill team and its supporters had agreed to meet on the village green at half-past one. Due to the short distance needed to travel – less than two miles – many of them were making their own way to the match. It being a fine day, they had decided to walk.

The team bus was a Leyland Cub – a former London Transport Country coach – which Barry Dick had mysteriously acquired during the war years. It had retained its green livery, though the name of its previous owners had been crudely painted out. It had clearly seen better days, but it served its purpose, and by the time the old bus had chuntered up alongside the pond opposite The Black Pig, most of the team were in attendance.

Alf Fortune, the team 'organiser', was beginning to fret, fingering his grimy notebook. 'Has anyone seen Tim?

'Not since last night,' answered Billy. 'Somebody said they saw him wandering off up the hill arm-in-arm with the two posh bints from London.'

'Very inconsiderate. Bloody typical!' moaned Alf, scratching his face as he always did when agitated. A quick head count revealed three of the team's 11 were missing – Tim, Tarquin, and Charlie.

'Tark's going from home, I presume, in his jam jar,' reported Ken, 'probably giving Charlie a lift from the manor house.' Ken was bringing his whole family along, which included his son Ivan, pencilled in as eleventh man, his long-suffering wife Olive, and his daughters Sasha and Jemima.

'We might as well get on,' griped Ted Jolly. 'Tim knows where the ground is. We've all been there often enough.'

They all began to pile on the coach; Hazel, with her father and dog Henry, was carrying a basket of apples, covered by a cloth. Sniffing some free food, Billy had a peek inside and was warned off in no uncertain fashion.

'They're fer later,' she said, sitting down on the seat next to Wally and smiling at him in a way that seemed to annoy Billy. She was still wearing her Sunday best dress and bonnet, and her cheeks were red and flushed. Wally was looking apprehensive, as he always did before a game. 'Getting' a bit windy, Wol?' she laughed.

Wally said nothing and looked out of the window as Barry fired up the old bus, its engine coughing noisily into life. He preferred to keep his thoughts to himself at times like this. Barney the dog lay at his feet and grumbled as the bus lurched forward and stalled with a judder.

'Come on, Barry!' cried Ken. 'Get this crate moving.'

Eventually, to ironic cheers, the old vehicle moved off, heading up the gentle slope to Uddles Wood. The sun shone brightly through the windows, and the fields outside shimmered green, with shafts of sunlight falling through the gaps in the trees, briefly blinding some of the passengers. It would take no more than a few minutes to reach their destination, which was probably just as well, since the old charabanc felt like it was going to conk out at any minute. Barry crunched through the gears as the bus neared the summit of the hill, making it lurch violently.

'That moron can't even drive a bus properly,' griped Ted.

'Do you think we can do it?' asked Alf, his ruddy face turning to Ken on the seat behind.

'Do what, get there in one piece?' joked Ken.

'Win the game?'

'Of course we can win,' Ken exuded a confidence he hardly felt. 'Listen, if Gordon Richards can win the Derby after 28 goes, and Stanley Matthews can finally win a cup-winners' medal after all these years, then we can beat West Rotting at cricket, can't we? They've got 22 arms and legs, same as us.'

'And climb Everest,' added Alf.

'Yeah, that too.'

'Actually, they've only got 21 legs,' stated Wally, whimsically.

'Eh?'

'You're forgetting Cedric,' laughed Ken.

'What's 'e on about?' grinned Hazel, nudging Wally.

The bus finally emerged from the woods and a long, sweeping valley spread out before them, with the tall steeple of the Christ Church instantly visible in the distance. Until the turn of the century, the village of West Rotting had been little more than a hamlet, but due to its position on the main B-road that joined the London to the south coast arterial road to the west, and the town of Tumbledon to the east, several lavish houses had been built there between the wars, with a few cheaper homes following in their wake. The village had flourished for the very reasons that Rotting Hill had become isolated and forgotten – transport communications. Even in these austere times, it retained an affluence that Rotting Hill could never hope to aspire to, and thereby lay the crux of the rivalry between the villages.

'I 'ope today won't end up in a bundle like the darts match,' chuckled Alf.

'If it does, it won't be our fault, mate,' returned Ken, remembering the occasion all too well, since he had ended up with a split lip.

The old bus took its time meandering along the winding road that led into the village, and then out the other side where the cricket ground was situated. As the coach crunched its way into the little car park by the side of the club pavilion, there were already figures in white throwing balls around and inspecting the wicket.

'They're keen buggers,' chirped Alf as the coach shunted to a halt, throwing everyone forward in their seats.

'Very enjoyable drive,' moaned Ted sarcastically, warming to his usual petulant pre-match mood.

The passengers piled off the bus, including three dogs and several children, just avoiding Jimmy Catt's screeching MG as it raced into the car park.

'Flash git!' snarled Ted. 'He'll kill somebody one day!'

Cedric Winford-Harvey was there to greet the arrivals, full of bonhomie. He knew almost everyone by name and greeted the players with a hearty handshake, including Wally, whom he always addressed as 'W.G.' – his second name being George.

'Jolly good luck. Nice to see you. Hope you're all shipshape. Anchors away at two on the dot.'

Despite his disability, the Commodore looked every inch a proper cricketer, dressed in a club cap and a blazer of green and purple stripes, topped with a pristine white choker about his neck. He was a man of slightly less than average height, but stocky and muscular in his upper body, much as he must have been in his youth.

Alf was somewhat disheartened to see the youthful Michael Mellors loosening up athletically in the outfield. He gazed around, hoping to see Tim Stewart, but there was no sign of him.

'Don't worry, mate, he'll turn up,' assured Ken, sensing his friend's anxiety.

Alf asked Cedric, 'Seen our skipper?'

'Afraid not, old boy. Can't say I have.'

As the team trundled their kit into the dressing room, Wally remarked on how full the ground looked already. The new pavilion was still adorned with the red, white, and blue bunting from Coronation Day. In front of the building, rows of deckchairs extended for about 20 yards on either side of the entrance. Along the shaded part of the ground, all the rough benches were occupied. Only the north side, bounded by the huge church steeple and a small row of cottage gardens, appeared empty.

'You're not expecting the Australians, are you?' quipped Barry, hauling his gear out of the coach and motioning towards the crowd.

'Good as, old boy,' returned Cedric playfully. 'Good as.'

In the changing room, lavishly furnished with padded seats, lockers, and showers, the Reverend Christian was becoming agitated. As nominal vice-captain of the team – a position accorded him more by his social rank than his tactical acumen, which was limited – he oversaw the side in the absence of Rupert St. Charles, who was nowhere to be seen.

'It really is a very poor show,' he frowned. 'Ten minutes before the off and he's not here yet. It's not on!'

''Old yer 'orses, Vic,' said Alf, pulling on pair of grubby white flannels, cobbled together with a series of off-white patches, ''E'll be 'ere.'

As if by magic, at that very moment Charlie stuck his head around the door, looking like a man with all the time in the world. 'Sorry, chaps,' he drawled. 'Tark's been searching for the ladies. Gone AWOL.'

Tarquin St. Charles sidled in nonchalantly behind his elder brother, looking slightly perturbed, though exuding the same laconic air – clearly a family trait. 'They'll be hell to pay if anything happens to Fiona. She's my boss's daughter, and I promised to keep an eye on her. She's inclined to run a bit wild if not kept on a short lead.'

'So, the girls didn't come home last night then?' asked Ken, winking at Ted.

'Don't worry, old chap,' grinned Charlie. 'They won't come to any harm around here. Everyone is very civilised. Anyone had a look at the wicket?'

'Well no, actually,' grimaced the Reverend. 'We were rather hoping you would have been here by now.'

'Don't see what difference that makes,' groused the permanently pessimistic Ted. 'We're going to lose anyway.'

'No sign of Tim, then?' asked Wally, practising a forward defensive stroke with his decrepit old bat.

'He's always late,' moaned Ted. 'He should be fined. That'd put a stop to it.'

'I think we should bat first if we win the toss,' suggested the vicar. 'It looks like being a hot one.'

'Charlie never wins the toss,' complained Ted, securing his flannels around his waist with an old tie.

'Ready to spin up, old boy?' Cedric asked, poking his head round the door.

'Two minutes,' retuned Charlie.

'I say, looks like Her Ladyship has turned up,' observed the home captain. 'Isn't that her grey Bentley?' Cedric pointed to the car park, where an oddly dressed middle-aged woman was being helped out of the car by a chauffeur.

'Oh yikes, it's Mama!' exclaimed Tarquin. 'What's she doing here?'

Outside the pavilion, Hazel parked herself down in the seat next to Daphne at the scorers' table. 'Afternoon, dear,' she chirped.

Daphne, now in a flowery dress in her favourite colour of orange and wearing a smart matching bonnet and sunglasses, glanced disdainfully up at her fellow scorer for the day, as Hazel produced her team's grubby, dog-eared scorebook and a pencil from her bag.

'Oh, hello,' returned Daphne snootily, with a look of, *oh God, I've got to put up with the likes of you all day*, on her face. 'Nice day.' She did not care much for Hazel, whom she thought rather common.

Hazel was going to enjoy their encounter, grinning inwardly as she made herself comfortable.

'Good luck, Cedric,' announced Daphne, as the two captains walked out to the middle to toss up, Cedric somewhat stiffly.

'They're only goin' to toss fer batting,' stated Hazel, in her best matter-of-fact tone.

'Yes, I'm quite aware of that actually, thank you very much.' Daphne lifted her sunglasses to give Hazel a condescending glare. Even though she was looking up at Hazel, who was slightly taller, she gave the impression of looking down her nose. It was going to be a difficult few hours.

'D'you wanna fag?' Hazel produced a packet of cigarettes and a box of matches from her bag.

'No, thank you very much. I find it most distracting whilst I'm scoring.'

'Don't mind if I do then, seeing as the game ain't started yet.'

'If you must, but over there, if you don't mind.' Daphne gestured towards the balcony of the pavilion.

Charlie and Cedric returned from the pitch, having shaken hands, the former looking rather gloomy not to mention somewhat shabby, compared to his opposite number.

'Don't tell me, we're fielding,' moaned Ted. 'I'll get the pads on.'

'Afraid so, chaps,' winced Charlie. 'Timmy rolled up yet?' No-one answered in the affirmative. 'Come on then, let's get out there. Billy, you take first over.'

Under the shade of the big oak tree, in the corner of the ground, Colonel Bartington-Phypps sat on a bench in his usual pose: hands resting on his shooting stick, leaning stiffly forward, dressed in his Sunday best suit adorned with his war medals, topped with a black bowler hat. A familiar figure soon joined him, wearing a faded fawn jacket and matching trousers, green shirt and cloth cap, accompanied as ever by a mournful grey dog with floppy ears.

'Hello, Jack, old bean. Nice day for it,' barked the Colonel.

'Aye, that it is,' replied his friend. The dog rolled over and snorted.

'Looks like the Commodore's won the toss again. Should be a run feast against this shower, what?' ventured the Colonel. Jack Hurst said nothing and began to fire up his old pipe.

'Just as well we lost the toss,' griped Ted, as the Rotting Hill team took the field to polite applause, tossing an old ball about, 'otherwise it'd be all over by teatime.'

'You really are a miserable old git. I don't know why you bother playing,' teased Barry Dick, performing a few arm exercises.

'And I don't know why you bother doing that,' parried Ted. 'Can't remember the last time you took a wicket.'

Just at that moment, a loud yell came from the far side of the ground and Caroline and Fiona came bounding in at the back gate, closely followed by Tim Stewart in his cricket whites.

'Cooee, Tark! Tark, it's me, cooee!' cried Fiona, looking a mite dishevelled.

'Oh cripes, they look well oiled,' whined Tarquin.

'Top and bottom, I shouldn't doubt,' grinned Charlie. 'You better go and get them settled. We don't want them showing us up.'

'I won't be a minute,' said his brother, scuttling away.

'Right then, come on, chaps.' Charlie clapped his hands lazily. 'Billy to bowl; Wally, slip; Chris, silly mid-off;

Ken, gully; Alf, cover; Barry, mid-on. If you please, gentlemen. I'll take mid-off. If Tim's ready in time, he can take next over. On your toes, everybody.'

To more enthusiastic applause, the West Rotting opening batsmen now took the field. The sun was shining, the birds were singing, the unusually large crowd was in its shirt sleeves, summer dresses, and bonnets. God was in his heaven. It was Sunday afternoon at the village cricket match. The nearby church clock struck two o'clock.

Chapter Ten

August 23rd 2pm

CEDRIC

The two West Rotting opening batsmen strode out to the wicket to great applause. At least, one of them did; Cedric Winford-Harvey's prosthetic limb made striding somewhat difficult – less a stride, more a shuffle. His partner, Neville Dodds – a lean, angular man in his late thirties – walked slowly alongside his captain, if not slightly behind, so as not to embarrass him.

Cedric's disability had never held him back on the cricket field, except perhaps to the extent that he could no longer bowl. He still insisted on opening the batting, as he had done before the war, and since he was the captain, no-one dared query this decision. In the circumstances, the long-suffering Dodds was somewhat restricted by this partnership, as running between the wickets was a painful and often tricky operation with Cedric at the other end. Consequently, Neville's perfectly executed leg glances and on-drives, those that failed to reach the boundary, could never be worth more than one run. Neville, a cautious player by nature, was often having to hit out boldly early in the innings to keep the scoreboard moving.

Opponents too, were by tradition generous to Cedric. His 'run' singles, accompanied by the cry of 'Just the jolly old one, Neville' never ended in the run outs they should have done, and at the commencement of his innings he was offered a charitable selection of long hops and full tosses by the opening bowlers, so he might accumulate a few cheap runs. His foot movement being restricted to virtually nothing, he would be defeated by any delivery of half-decent pace. The general form was therefore to give Cedric a few easy runs to save face, then dismiss him when the pantomime had gone on long enough, whereat he would depart the field to stentorian acclaim with 10 or 12 against his name in the scorebook, honour and ego satisfied. Once this farce had ended, the contest would begin in earnest. Any opposition deviating from this policy soon found themselves aimed off the fixture list in short order.

As the batsman took guard – Cedric always by tradition received the first ball – Daphne began to fill in the virgin page of her scorebook.

West Rotting CC v Rotting Hill CC
Played at – West Rotting
Date – Sunday, August 23rd, 1953
Start time – 2pm
Toss won by – West Rotting

These items she filled in with ordinary pencil. The names of the batsmen were then entered in different colours – C.A. Winford-Harvey in orange; Dodds N.D. in green.

'Moon bowlin' first, dear,' stated Hazel, as Billy was thrown the bright red ball, which he began rubbing into his groin.

'Yes, I can see that, actually,' snapped back Daphne, having now replaced her sunshades with her secretarial spectacles.

'Why do they do that?' asked Hazel.

'I'm sorry, do what?'

'Rub themselves with the ball like that.'

Daphne sniffed. 'I have absolutely no idea. Shall we get on with it?'

Cedric was taking an inordinately long time marking out his crease. 'Two legs please, old boy,' meaning a middle to leg stump guard, he barked to the umpire, who happened to be Reg Barclay. The terms of engagement for these friendly encounters decreed that each side should provide one umpire, who may or may not necessarily be one of the players.

'That's a bit optimistic,' joked Ted, in a rare moment of humour.

'He means middle and leg,' confirmed Wally, standing next to Ted at slip.

'Yes, I did know that,' growled the wicket keeper.

'I'd 'ave thought "leg stump" would be more appropriate,' chimed a grinning Ken.

'Shut up, he'll hear you,' admonished Wally.

If Cedric did hear, he took no notice, proceeding to bang his bat into the ground, creating clouds of dust. Reg Barclay had been confirmed at number 11 on the Commodore's batting order – handed to Daphne prior to the game – and was therefore the natural choice for umpiring duties. He enjoyed the process, thinking himself an expert in the rules of the game and a natural arbiter of fair play. He was still feeling peeved by the fact he had not been automatic choice for the game and had only been roped in when someone else cried off. Not only that, but he was not considered worthy enough to bat higher in the order than someone not sporting a full set of legs. Of course, he was not alone in this respect, but his own single-mindedness, and the captain's apparent cavalier disregard for his position within the club, was a dangerous combination fomenting in his intensely active brain.

Reg carefully manoeuvred Cedric's bat into the approximate position required, whereupon the batsman began banging his bat into the crease yet again, then scuffing up the line with the boot of his good foot, creating more clouds of dust, some of which was blown on the breeze towards the fielders behind the wicket. He then gazed about the ground, deliberately counting the number of fielders, then balanced himself comfortably, ready to receive the first ball.

'Get on with it!' griped Ted, eager to get the game going, as Billy had to abort his run-up when Cedric prevaricated yet again. Cedric turned to give the 'keeper a withering look, then returned to his guard.

The batsman finally settled, as did the fielders. Reg lifted his left arm out sideways, as if directing traffic. Then, satisfied at last that everything was ready, he called out in time-honoured fashion, 'Play.'

It was a defining moment, as is the first ball of every cricket match: the batsman stands ready, the bowler prepares to bowl, the fielders crouch down or move in from their distant positions. The possibilities are infinite; no two matches could ever be the same. The spectators hushed in anticipation.

Billy Moon did not take a long run-up to the wicket; in fact, he barely took a run-up at all, ambling in a couple of paces and whipping the ball at the batsman, all the strength and momentum emanating from his powerful shoulders. Opponents who'd never seen him before were frequently taken by surprise with the pace of the ball, accompanied by a loud grunt from the bowler.

The first ball passed harmlessly down the leg side, as wicket keeper Ted Jolly stopped it clumsily with his pads.

'No ball!' yelled Reg, theatrically extending his arm – the given signal to the scorers.

'What for?' queried the bemused bowler.

'Not advising mode of delivery,' stated Reg in his best professional voice.

'Eh?'

'He means how you are going to bowl,' pointed out Charlie from mid-off.

'What do you mean, "how I'm going to bowl"?'

'Right arm, over the wicket, umpire,' Charlie instructed, grinning.

'Eh?'

'Thank you, gentlemen,' added Reg. 'Continue.'

'Just get on with it!' Ted snapped.

The bowler, decidedly irked by the turn of events, whizzed the next delivery down at least two yards quicker, whipping in from the off side and just eluding Cedric's stiff prod forward, missing the stumps by a whisker. An audible gasp passed around the ground.

'Well bowled, old boy!' gasped the startled batsman, expecting his usual gentle full toss or long hop to get off the mark.

'Steady on,' commanded Charlie, throwing the ball back to Billy.

'I'm just givin' 'im a few warning shots across the bowels,' advised Billy, his cricketing feathers ruffled by Reg's pedantry, as the fielders laughed at a typical Moon malapropism.

The visitors were clearly not sticking to the usual script, or perhaps had forgotten about it. Two more similar deliveries followed, both quicker and slanting back into the batsman, the second of which caught Cedric a nasty blow to the groin, causing another murmur around the ground. This was clearly not going to be the usual friendly game of cricket the patrons were used to.

Billy's next ball straightened and kept low, striking the West Rotting captain on his front pad – rather pointlessly protecting his artificial leg – with a loud 'clonk'. 'How was that?' cried the bowler, turning to the umpire more in hope than expectation.

Now, it was an unwritten law at West Rotting, like allowing Cedric a few easy runs, that no umpire ever gave the captain out leg before wicket, especially if the offending ball had struck his synthetic limb. No-one had ever dared give such a decision so, with this in mind, Cedric cursed briefly, then resumed his batting stance awaiting the next ball, only to see Reg standing stiffly to attention, his right index finger raised in the air.

'Great bowling, Billy!' cried Alf, running in to congratulate the bowler, as the Commodore stood in disbelief, staring up the wicket at Reg.

'What's going on?' Cedric enquired.

'I'm afraid he's given you out, old boy,' chuckled Charlie, picking up the ball which had rebounded a considerable distance down the wicket.

'What!'

'Sorry, skip, absolutely plumb,' confirmed Reg, in his best neutral tone.

'WHAT!'

Cedric glared at Reg for a moment, cursed loudly, then tucked his bat under his arm and limped painfully, perhaps a little too painfully, back towards the pavilion, passing Reg as he did so. 'You nincompoop!' he cursed, as he glared at the miscreant arbiter. 'I'll speak to you later, harrumph!' followed by what sounded like 'You spunksoaked pissbucket!' Cedric was known to swear in combinations of bodily effluence and receptacles when angered.

Back on the boundary, Daphne sat stunned, as indeed did most of the spectators. Only the Rotting Hill contingent applauded, though somewhat embarrassingly, as this kind of behaviour was somehow unprecedented. As Cedric hobbled past her, Daphne turned and gazed sorrowfully, tears forming in her eyes. 'Bad luck, Cedric,' she murmured as he passed.

But Cedric did not hear. He stumbled up the pavilion steps, mumbling something about wankpots and pisspans. From inside the dressing-room came the sound of more profanities and possibly a bat being thrown.

'Right, so that's Winford-Harvey, l.b.w. bowled Moon for nought,' chuckled Hazel, gleefully filling in the details in her own grubby scorebook.

'What?' whimpered Daphne.

'Aren't yer goin' to fill in yer nice book, dear? That's one wicket for one run, ain't it?'

Daphne was not really listening, her face a picture of sadness. It was bad enough that poor Cedric should lose his leg in the service of his country in the prime of life, and that he was being cuckolded by some jumped-up, bogus war hero with his bitch of a wife, but now he had been given out without even a run by the husband of her best friend. Life was so unfair. Pulling a handkerchief from her dress pocket, she blew her nose violently.

'Bit of a turn-up, eh?' grinned Hazel.

'Don't worry, there's plenty of batting to come,' responded her fellow scorer, pulling herself together.

Chapter Eleven

August 23rd 2.15pm

TIM

Daphne was quite right: the cream of the West Rotting batting was still to come. The Commodore's replacement was Archie Duncan, a tall bespectacled Scotsman in his early forties, the headmaster of Tumbledon Grammar School. He was clearly a man who brooked no nonsense and strode to the wicket with a great sense of purpose. His fierce countenance concealed a somewhat gentler and more sensitive nature, but any improper behaviour, whether perpetrated by his pupils or fellow sportsmen, was immediately condemned as 'unacceptable', 'completely unacceptable', or in the most extreme cases 'totally unacceptable'. Daphne entered his name in red pencil.

Accompanying him onto the field of play was, by a quirk of fate, one of his former pupils. Timothy Alexander Stewart – the only member of the Rotting Hill team (bar young Ivan Kippax) not old enough to have fought in the war. Tim had good cause to remember Archie, who had been a maths master when he gave him a good beating ten years previously, just prior to being expelled for smoking, drinking, and getting a member of the nearby girls' school pregnant. Tim had been a member of the school's first eleven and might well have become a very useful cricketer had he not chosen to pursue a life of debauchery instead. His sexual exploits had become known far and wide, with mothers tending to lock their daughters away when he appeared in the vicinity.

Having now changed into his cricket boots, Tim ran onto the field just in time to bowl the first over from the church end, accompanied by a good deal of clapping and shrieking from Fiona and Caroline, who had requisitioned a couple of deckchairs and seated themselves by the mid-wicket boundary. Umpire Reg Barclay had forbidden him to enter the field until the end of the first over, which left him clicking his heels in mild frustration, and then started quibbling as to whether Tim was eligible to bowl, as he had not been on the field at the start of play. This prompted wicket keeper Ted Jolly to call out, 'Get stuffed!' and 'Shove it up your hole!', causing Reg to relent his pedantry, following a conciliatory intervention from Bert Fisher, his fellow umpire.

Tim began to mark out his run-up, which seemed inordinately long, almost to the boundary. It was always a graceful and athletic approach to the wicket, though by the time he reached the stumps to deliver the ball, it was projected down the pitch at little more than medium pace. In truth, Tim probably bowled slower than Billy, but the batsmen were conned into thinking he was going to bowl fast, and that was the trick, though he could work up quite a generous pace on a hard, flat wicket, and would require little encouragement to pitch a couple of short balls at his former schoolmaster. He was, however, inclined to be erratic – 'a loose popgun' as his captain Charlie once described him with his usual laconic eloquence.

'Come on, Timmy, knock his bails off!' hooted Fiona, as Tim's wiry frame hurled down the first ball. It swung wildly away down the leg side, eluding Ted's feeble grope, and ran away for four byes. It was an over best forgotten, as the bowler already looked on the verge of collapse and was rested shortly after in favour of Charlie's gentle leg-cutters.

After the initial shock of Cedric's demise, the innings settled down to a more predictable pattern, as the Rotting Hill bowlers offered up their usual assortment of long hops, full tosses, and other rubbish, to which Dodds and Duncan took full advantage. Neville Dodds, mercifully released from having to bat with his encumbered captain, was now able to play his naturally cautious game, though even he could not fail to make hay in this sunshine. The scoreboard soon began to click around with a greater rapidity, allowing the patrons to settle down to the usual entertainment.

Tim had now been banished to the mid-wicket boundary, which gave him plenty of opportunity to show off in front of his new lady fans, whilst at the same time attempting to sober up. He briefly disappeared into the bushes by the groundsman's shed to relieve his bladder. The introduction of Wally's leg breaks into the attack generally meant more employment for the boundary fielders, and this day was no exception. However, one of his juicy long hops induced a miscue from Dodds, which sailed skywards in Tim's direction. Despite the fielder's somewhat frail condition, together with the fact he had barely had time to button up his flannels, Tim caught the ball effortlessly on the run, rolling over several times to spectacular effect, before throwing the captured orb high in celebration. This brought the girls to their feet in wild applause and even wilder whooping, accompanied by more sedate clapping from the rest of the ground.

The scoreboard now read –
Total 47 Wickets 2 Last Man 21

New batsman Jimmy Catt now strode nonchalantly to the wicket, dressed much like his skipper in a purple and green cap and white choker. Jimmy fancied himself as West Rotting's Denis Compton – a flamboyant, devil-may-care type of batsman. He could not fail to notice Fiona and Caroline taking more than a passing interest in his arrival. Jimmy was not a man for playing himself in, thereby just as often recording a duck as a fifty. But despite his earlier encounter with Phyllis, he was feeling good, and there was a fair crowd for him to show off in front of. He got off the mark first ball with an elegant on-drive to the boundary, and proceeded to dominate the bowling from then on.

With runs now flowing freely at both ends, Charlie changed his bowlers around constantly. Ken Kippax was offered a couple of overs with his slow left-armers, but after one long hop went sailing into the adjoining field for six, he invoked the shrapnel wound and asked to be relieved. The Reverend Christian, with his higher delivery, achieved a modicum of turn with his off-breaks, but Barry Dick – an erratic bowler at the best of times – was having the usual problems with his direction. A whole overs' worth sailed down the leg side, causing much frustration from batsman Archie Duncan and wicket keeper Ted Jolly, who finally gave up trying to stop the ball and let it run away for byes.

'Bowl at the fucking stumps, you cretin!' wuffled Ted, from under his faded brown cap and the thick gumshield that he wore.

'Don't blame me for your incompetence,' returned Barry. 'Try stopping the ball with your big nose. Nothing else seems to be much use.'

'Shut up, you gyppo!'

'Sheep molester!'

'Gentlemen, please moderate your language,' pleaded umpire Fisher, who up to this point had been dozing lazily in the sunshine. His back was beginning to play up, as it always did when things got a bit hairy out in the middle.

'What!' snarled Ted. 'What did he call me!'

'Now come on, chaps,' implored Charlie, doing his captain's bit as he walked around gently clapping his hands.

The banter had not died down by the time the vicar trundled in to deliver the first ball of the next over, causing a now highly agitated Archie to step away from the crease in annoyance. 'Could ye please keep the chat doon,' he growled in his thick Glaswegian accent. 'This is totally unacceptable. I cannae concentrate properly. This is a cricket match, no' a debating society.'

Chris bowled the next ball and then stood grimacing, hand on hips, as Archie swung it away for four runs to square leg. This familiar pose was humorously known as 'The Vicar's Teapot' and normally signalled the start of a rather childish bout of sulking.

Ken Kippax was also not in good humour. He was hoping another wicket might fall so he could have a crafty fag, and was now beginning to drift, a phenomenon that always occurred when the tide began to turn against Rotting Hill. Ken would be posted to his usual fielding position – either point or gully – where he would serve with much enthusiasm until things started to go wrong, when he would then begin to 'drift' towards the nearest fielder to complain about something, most commonly the bowling or Charlie's captaincy. Invariably, the ball would then trace a path from the bat through the area which Ken had just vacated, generally at catchable height – not that anything at catchable height was likely to be caught by Ken, who was blind as a bat. He would spill the simplest of offerings, but paradoxically cling onto anything moving at the speed of light, after which he would throw the captured ball dismissively in the air before embarking on a lap of honour around the field.

Meanwhile Jimmy, much to the admiration of his newly-found female admirers, was treating the bowling with the contempt it deserved, and the hundred total was reached for the loss of only two wickets, amidst great applause from the spectators.

'Going quite well now,' purred Daphne, somewhat smugly, as she posted another four against Catt J. M., suitably in black pencil. Hazel ignored her.

The Commodore stood stiffly nearby, puffing on his pipe, having now recovered his composure. 'Full speed ahead, eh, Daffers?' he beamed.

'Full speed ahead, skipper,' she repeated gaily.

'Fancy an apple, luv?' asked Hazel, trying to appear unimpressed.

Back on the field, the Rotting Hill team were becoming a little frayed at the edges – not unusual at this stage of an opposition innings. Ted Jolly was griping away incomprehensively through his gum shield behind the stumps; the Reverend Christian was frantically teapotting and sighing deeply; Ken was way adrift, standing next to his son at cover point; Billy continuously exclaimed, 'Oh, my word!' every time the ball whistled past him in the field; Tim, marooned in the outfield, was cursing loudly at every run and kicking imaginary balls along the grass. The rest of the team were getting hot under the collar, apart from Charlie and Tarquin, casually taking the world in their stride.

Jimmy Catt on-drove the vicar for another perfectly executed boundary, at which point the tins on the scoreboard signalled 50 against his number. Huge applause rang out around the ground as he gave a regal wave of his bat and doffed his cap in recognition. Becoming bored with the ease of it all, and keen to check out his female admirers, who had now disappeared into the bar for a top-up, he proceeded to throw his wicket away by having a huge heave at the next ball, then glaring in mock horror at the shattered stumps behind him.

He trudged off the field to another loud round of applause. 'Well batted,' complimented Charlie, as Jimmy passed him on the way back to the pavilion.

'Yeah, piss off, you flash ponce,' crackled Ted, retrieving the scattered bails.

Jimmy was replaced by Peregrine Hacker (blue pencil), who was very likely to have been the fattest man ever to play cricket. A tax inspector by profession, Hacker was almost as wide as he was tall, and it seemed an anatomical miracle that he was even able to walk, never mind scamper up and down between the wickets. Nevertheless, this portly figure hid a surprisingly athletic bent which was more than capable of increasing the score with much rapidity. The bat looked like a toy in his huge, flabby hands, but it wasn't long before it was smashing the ball all around the park, if in a slightly ungainly manner. At a few minutes past four o'clock in the afternoon, the scorebook registered:

Total 152 Wickets 3 Last Man 52

By now the Rotting Hillers had lost all sense of discipline, arguing amongst themselves, sniping at each other, misfielding, and throwing the ball in all over the place, much to Ted's increasing annoyance. A rout was in the offing; at the very least, a score of well over 200. Charlie, never the most reactive of captains, in the tactical sense, realised that he had to slow the game down somehow or the opposition would run riot. Like all leaders, he always took the blame when things went wrong, though rarely got any credit for positive results. He was seriously now considering bringing Tim back on to bowl.

The young rascal had been fermenting on the boundary for most of the innings. The popsies had tired of his antics, as had most of the spectators in the vicinity, having endured a barrage of profanities in the last hour, mostly aimed at his captain and team colleagues. A mother had removed herself and her two young children to a quieter part of the ground after Tim had vomited in the nearby bushes, and an elderly lady, having berated him for his foul language, was told to 'Shut up, you old hag!' for her impudence. He was now becoming so browned off with proceedings that he seriously considered walking off the field altogether to see where Fiona and Caroline had disappeared to. The vicar had sat himself down on a nearby bench, still sulking, and cleaning some imaginary mud from the spikes of his cricket boots.

A curious incident then occurred which changed the course of events. Henry, the Fishers' Old English Sheepdog, suddenly wandered onto the field of play, all the way up to the wicket without being noticed, and calmly cocked his leg up against the stumps at the pavilion end and urinated, which everyone found extremely amusing. Everyone except umpire Reg Barclay, who immediately shouted out, 'Get that fucking dog off the pitch!' The outburst was heard by everyone on the ground, who all stopped laughing and went very quiet.

'Sorry, chaps,' bleated a rueful Bert Fisher. 'He's only a pup. Henry, get away!' He pointed the errant dog back towards the pavilion as Hazel called out his name, but the hairy beast just stood staring at his master.

Reg, standing behind the set of stumps that had just been defiled, aimed a kick in the dog's direction, whereupon Henry, normally the most placid of creatures, jumped up, growled, and began to move threateningly towards the umpire, who had to backpedal so rapidly that he fell over on his backside, much to everyone's amusement.

All this proved great ammunition for Tim, who immediately exclaimed, 'Put the dog on to bowl. He can't do any worse than you lot!' Pleased with his latest contribution, which provoked much chuckling, he immediately added, 'And don't forget to tell the umpire his action – right paw over the wicket!'

The fielders all laughed like drains. Reg, however, having just avoided being savaged as Henry ran back to the pavilion, did not see the funny side of it. Neither did batsman Archie Duncan, mumbling away that it was all 'completely unacceptable'.

Nevertheless, this strange episode upset the momentum of the game. Tim was immediately recalled to the attack as Charlie sensed a change in the ambience as the match took a new turn. Angry at being neglected for so long, put out to grass on the boundary, and fired up by not only a whole series of imagined grievances but also the total incompetence of his colleagues, he now roared in to bowl on a pitch that was beginning to cut up and be unpredictable. Archie, up to that point exuding confidence and totally in control, suddenly began to feel apprehensive. He prodded limply at Tim's next delivery, which spat, took the edge of his bat, and arced its way to Wally at first slip, who clumsily dropped it. Tim's momentum had carried him almost the whole way down the wicket, and he let out a deafening expletive that could probably be heard as far away as Tumbledon. The arena went quiet again.

Wally mewled an apology and avoided eye contact with any of his teammates. Ever since waking up that morning, he had had this strange feeling that today was going to be a special day, that something good was going to happen and he would be a major player in it. This sensation had nagged and tugged at him, although it did not appear to be bearing fruition. Already his bowling had been smashed all over the park, and now he had put down a simple catch. He kept thinking of Hazel, scribbling away in her scorebook on the boundary, winding up that stuffy Daphne woman.

Notwithstanding, Archie was rattled. Flapping at Tim's next ball, he missed completely and heard the death rattle of the stumps behind him as Tim let out a loud whoop of satisfaction. Totally against the previous flow of the day, the West Rotting innings suddenly went into collapse mode. Billy was brought back on at the other end, and wickets began to tumble with regularity. Not only that, but the runs started to dry up as well. Cedric was getting twitchy back at H.Q., whilst Daphne had to rapidly rotate her coloured pencils as the batsmen came and went.

Because of this, Reg had to be relieved of his umpiring duties by the Commodore, who took his place. Having checked into the kitchen to ensure Doreen was all systems go with the teas, he began to fall into a state of more agitation. Wickets were falling, and there was still some time to go before a possible declaration.

One of the reasons Cedric offered to umpire at the latter stages of an innings was that he was in a perfect position to monitor the state of the game and coach his batsmen as thought necessary. This conduct was, of course, generally accepted to be against the spirit of cricket, but the West Rotting skipper, along with many other aspects, was seemingly allowed a good deal of latitude in this area – no other team having ever complained about it.

Reg had not had a bat for more than a month. In truth, he was not much of a batsman, or any kind of cricketer: his eyesight was not that great and his physical co-ordination little better. But then, Cedric only had one leg! As the seventh West Rotting wicket fell, Reg started to scuff around urgently in the team's kitbag for a decent pair of leg pads and batting gloves. It was still only half-past four, and Cedric was never known to declare the innings much before five. He might just get a few minutes' batting.

Inside the pavilion, up at the bar, Fiona and Caroline had made the acquaintance of Jimmy Catt, who was soon accounting in heroic detail his bogus wartime exploits in the RAF. Back on the field of play, Tim, totally unaware that his lothario status was being usurped, was now working up a fair pace and skittling his way through the West Rotting tailenders. For once, Charlie's tactical ploy had worked; the longer run-up of his bowler, and the now frequent change of batting personnel, had virtually brought the scoreboard to a halt.

Cedric was becoming a trifle agitated as he handed out advice to his remaining batsmen. 'Hit out, chaps, declaring in a minute. Perry, try hitting him over mid-wicket, there's a big gap there.'

'Oi, excuse me!' broke in Ted. 'You're supposed to be umpiring, not telling the batsmen what to do.'

'Harrumph!' coughed Cedric, not used to being rebuked in this way on a cricket field by what he considered a bunch of peasant yokels. It was bad enough that they had not observed the usual courtesies and got him out for a duck, but now these upstarts were questioning his sportsmanship. *If they weren't such a pushover*, he thought, looking slightly embarrassed, *they'd be off the fixture list damn quick at the next AGM.*

At precisely 20 minutes to five, West Rotting's ninth wicket fell. The grotesque Peregrine Hacker had been flailing at the ball for a while and puffing and panting between the wickets for the best part of an hour. His face was now completely crimson, and sweat was pouring from his bloated head in waterfalls. Carrying his toy bat in one hand and a sodden handkerchief in the other, he now looked as if he was about to drop dead from exhaustion or cardiac arrest at any moment. It was therefore almost a blessed relief when he took a tired swing at Billy Moon and heard the crash of the stumps behind him.

Back on the boundary, Reg, girding up his loins, took a deep breath, pushed his glasses back up his nose, tucked his bat under his arm, and strode manfully out on to the pitch. Not until he had reached about halfway to the wicket, did he become aware of figures in white passing him going in the opposite direction.

'Where are you off to?' growled Cedric, coming face to face with Reg. 'I've just declared, you dozy snotbucket. Don't you ever pay attention!' The Commodore was clearly not in good humour, having not only seen his once dominant team collapse, but also having been taken to task for what he deemed perfectly acceptable behaviour.

Reg stood flabbergasted. There seemed no logical reason why he should not have been allowed to go in to bat and complete the innings: the score was only 178-9, and it was not yet teatime. But Cedric was a man well known for holding grudges; Reg had given him out leg before wicket, and this was his revenge. For a brief moment, Reg stood in the middle of the park all alone, looking bewildered, until realising how silly he looked. Inwardly fuming, he reluctantly turned and followed the other cricketers into the pavilion for their tea.

Back at the scorers' table, Hazel observed, 'That's a turn up f' the book, ain't it?'

'Not at all,' sniffed Daphne. 'I'm sure the captain knows what he's doing.'

Chapter Twelve

August 23rd 4.45pm

TEA

Over by the old oak tree, Colonel Bartington and Jack Hurst were deep in conversation.

'Should've brought young 'un back on earlier,' mused Jack.

'Bit of a collapse, what?' expressed the Colonel.

'Told yer,' Jack added, 'this lot's better than they look. Village team 'ad better watch out.'

'Oh, I don't think so, old boy. Haven't got any decent batsmen, as I recall. Nothing much to worry about.'

The conversation then drifted around to the recent Test series between England and Australia, with the Colonel expounding his pet subject of professional captains. 'I'm sorry, old chap, but it just isn't done. England's captain should always be an amateur. That's how it's always been, and I see no reason to change. That

Hutton chappie just isn't up to the job; look how he ran himself out the other evening.'

'Don't talk daft,' retorted Jack, ''e were best batsman in series.'

'Of course,' pointed out the Colonel, gravitating quickly away from an argument he looked like losing, 'Wally Hammond was a professional, you know.'

'Aye, but 'e 'ad to turn amateur to get England captaincy. Bloody ridiculous!'

'Naturally, but at least he did the decent thing.'

'Soom say 'e were a blackie, y'know,' suggested Jack, mischievously. 'Dark an' swarthy, 'e were, and 'ad a passion fer the ladies. It were said 'e couldn't keep 'is cock in 'is pocket.'

'What utter rot!' stormed back the Colonel, giving Jack a contemptuous glare, never failing to rise to his companion's impertinent bait. 'Do you really think he would have been elected captain of England if he was a darkie? Why, even the West Indies don't have a darkie as captain. It just isn't done.'

'Aye, but It's coomin'. Just you mark my words.'

'You really do talk some drivel sometimes, Jack. I wonder whether you really understand anything about cricket at all.' The Colonel rose stiffly to his feet. 'Fancy a cuppa, old chap?'

'Aye, gerrus a cuppa tea and a bun, thank y'kindly.'

The old soldier marched briskly off, as if he was on the parade ground.

'Silly ol' booger,' muttered Jack, once his friend was out of earshot.

*

Back in the pavilion, Doreen and Daphne were scurrying around busily serving the teas.

'Oh, my word!' exclaimed Billy, when he saw the piles of sandwiches, cakes, and other goodies piled up on the long table, which could seat all 22 players, plus umpires and scorers. No sooner had he sat down than he was piling heaps of food into his mouth. 'Any chocolate cake?' he asked, stuffing a mince pie and a jam tart into his mouth at the same time.

'So, whaddya think our chances are?' asked Alf, to no-one in particular.

'Practically nil,' opined the eternally pessimistic Ted. 'I can't bat, for a start. I've pulled another muscle and busted at least two fingers. Don't fancy facing Young Mellors on that pitch.'

'You can't bat full time,' quipped Barry Dick. 'The scorer should fill in a permanent nought against your name, save having to write it in later.' Ted ignored him.

'Good job you lot weren't on the beaches at Normandy,' offered Ken, lighting a cigarette.

'Do you have to smoke at the tea table?' griped Ted.

Unlike most of the team, who were either displaced cockneys like Bert and Hazel, or were locals who spoke with a soft, undistinguished southern accent, Ken's dialect was neither north nor south, nor anything in-between. His family had originally come from Lincolnshire, though his parents had moved to London before the war. When his eldest son Ivan was born, right in the middle of the Luftwaffe's blitz on the capital, the Kippaxes were evacuated to the relative safety of the countryside, where they liked it so much they had remained ever since.

'What is he on about now?' grinned Charlie.

'Was that before or after you were wounded?' giggled Barry.

'Listen, mate,' returned Ken, stiffening in his chair and taking the cigarette out of his mouth to stuff in a cheese sandwich, 'you can be as sarky as you like, but if it wasn't for blokes like me, this country would be crawling with Germans by now.'

'So, who's opening then?' asked Wally, changing the subject, but hoping he wouldn't be asked.

'Same as usual. Alf and yours truly,' confirmed Charlie, pouring out a cup of tea from the huge pot.

'Erm, I actually don't feel like it today,' said Alf. 'Me back's playin' up a bit.'

'Nonsense,' beamed Charlie. 'You'll do a great job. I've got a feeling you'll get a 50 today.'

To the best of anyone's recollection, Alf Fortune had never scored a 50. In truth, he would do well to get ten, and was only bullied into opening the batting because no-one else would do it, especially with the thought of facing West Rotting's renowned young fast bowler Mellors.

'Yeah, if you don't run me out again,' sniffed Alf, recalling past disasters. Charlie was notorious for his poor calling and running between the wickets.

'So, what is the batting order then?' pressed Wally.

'Alf and I opening,' stated Charlie, with a mouthful of cake. 'Chris three, Tark four, then Tim and Wally. We'll see what the situation is after all that.'

'Put my boy in last,' Ken insisted. 'I don't want him facing Mellors. Everyone else'll 'ave to move up one.'

'I'm not sure we can negotiate that,' grinned Charlie. 'All right then. Barry seven, then Billy, Ken, and Ted.'

'I'm not batting,' moaned Ted. 'I told you. I'm injured.'

'I'm perfectly sure you'll have recovered by then.' There was the usual hint of sarcasm in Charlie's voice. 'Got that?'

Hazel, sitting opposite and busy scoffing a large chunk of sponge cake, nodded in silent agreement.

'How many do we need?' asked Wally.

'They got 178,' she replied, swallowing quickly.

'Less than usual,' stated Ken optimistically. 'Normally, they get about 230 against us.'

'Down to Tim,' observed Tarquin. 'Where is he, by the way?'

'Probably giving the popsies another pasting,' Ken laughed.

'Oh dear, I do hope not,' whined Tarquin. 'They don't usually behave like this. It must be the country air.'

'Feelin' confident, Wol?' Hazel enquired, heartily.

But Wally was feeling anything but confident, not having had a great day so far. In fact, he did not feel well at all, having a nervous pain in the groin and stomach, which he always got before an important innings, and which seemed particularly bad today. 'I think I'm going to pack it in at the end of the season,' he moaned. 'It's getting too much for me, all this running about.'

'Leave it out, Wol. Yer bin saying that for as long as I've known yer,' grinned Hazel. 'Yer don't look after yerself. Yer need feeding up properly; got years left in yer yet.'

Wally said nothing and took another sip of his tea. Hazel was smiling at him from across the table in an odd sort of way that made him feel uncomfortable. 'Got this feelin' you'll do something brilliant today.'

'I wish.'

'I'll tell you what gets my goat,' offered Ted, having run out of topics to moan about. 'Their bloody captain coaching his batsmen when he's umpiring. I thought that wasn't allowed.'

'I didn't know you had a goat,' said Billy, innocently. 'Where d'you keep it then?'

Wally grinned at Hazel, who smiled back between mouthfuls of cake.

'Oh, do me a favour, Bill! It's like bleedin' children's hour in 'ere,' sighed Ken, shaking his head. 'Come on, chaps, let's get out there.'

'What for?' queried Billy. 'We won't be needed to bat yet. Anyway, I 'aven't finished my tea.'

'Everything alright, boys?' asked a beaming Daphne, who had suddenly appeared and started clearing some of the empty plates.

Billy leered at her and said, 'Smashin grub, fit for the queen.'

'So glad you like it,' replied Daphne, routinely.

'Did you make it then?' asked Billy.

'Some of it. Myself and Doreen Barclay.'

Billy stared goggle-eyed at Daphne as she wiggled off with the empty plates.

'What are you gawping at?' asked Barry, sitting on Billy's right.

'She's a bit of alright, isn't she?'

'Stone me, Billy! 'Ow many years 'ave you bin comin' 'ere an' you've just noticed ol' Daphne,' said Hazel, looking a bit peeved.

Billy exchanged glances with her, immediately feeling like a chastised schoolboy – an exchange Wally couldn't help noticing. Billy realised he had somehow said the wrong thing but had no idea what.

'Come on, Bill, I'll toss you for first umpire,' said Ken.

'Eh?'

'Bert's back's playin' up. He needs a rest.'

Billy pushed back his chair and stood up, grabbing a handful of dog-eared sandwiches, and lurched out of the door, 'So, have you seen this goat Ted's got then?' he asked Ken as they walked off.

Everyone else had left the table, leaving Hazel and Wally on their own. He noticed she was looking a bit bothered. 'Has he upset you again?' he asked.

'Why should 'e 'ave upset me?' she bristled, going pink in the face.

'Hazel,' he whispered, leaning across the table, 'Billy only thinks from the waist down.'

She stared at him, scarcely believing what he had just said. 'An' why should that bovver me?'

'Well, I thought…'

'You thought what?'

'Well, you and Billy.'

'There is no me an' Billy, Wol, never 'as bin an' never will be. That good enough for yer?'

Looking crestfallen, Wally hung his head and mumbled, 'Sorry.'

He started to leave, but she grabbed his hand. 'Didn't mean t'snap at yer. Are yer alright?'

'Just a bit windy,' he laughed. 'Sorry I brought it up.'

'I'm jus' gonna 'ave a quick fag, then I'll be out. Sorry.' She shot him a weak smile.

Wally wandered outside, curious to what their latest exchange had meant. Hazel had been behaving strangely to him all weekend; he still had no idea what was going on.

There were still a few West Rotting players sitting at the opposite table, but most of them had hustled off to prepare for fielding. Hazel sat quietly brooding for a while, nibbling at the leftover food. In the kitchen, behind a serving hatch, she could see Daphne in her apron, organising a mousy little woman who she guessed was Doreen Barclay, Reg's wife.

She sniffed and rummaged in her dress pocket for her cigarettes and box of matches. *I could put on a better spread than this*, she thought, still watching Daphne. *What on earth does Billy see in her, the fat old cow?* She chided herself for thinking that way. After all, Billy meant nothing to her – or so she tried to convince herself. Wally clearly didn't like the thought of her and Billy, and she grinned at the notion of two silly men being jealous about her.

She could not take her eyes off Daphne. For a moment, their glances met, and Daphne flashed a frosty smile in Hazel's direction. Hazel smiled weakly back. 'Nice tea, dear.'

Daphne ignored her.

'Stuck up cow!' muttered Hazel and lit her cigarette.

Chapter Thirteen

August 23Rd 5.15pm

CHARLIE

By the time the Rotting Hill innings began, the sky had clouded over, and the temperature was a good deal cooler. Ken had lost the toss to umpire and was accompanied onto the field by openers Rupert St. Charles and Alf 'Lucky' Fortune.

Charlie looked anything but the potential eighteenth Earl of Ashfield, if that indeed was what he would someday become. He still had that aristocratic bearing that was his birthright, and he was certainly still quite handsome, though it was hard to notice beneath the lank, floppy hair, and several days' growth of beard. Nor would one have guessed it from his attire – a shabby pair of off-white cricket flannels with a tear at both knees, plus an equally faded red cap that seemed too small for his head. At 35, he was probably at his physical peak, but though it did not show outwardly, his experiences in the Spanish Civil War had left a profound mark on him.

He was now terrified of fast bowling, or indeed, any kind of possible physical injury. In Spain, he had witnessed some of his best friends and comrades blown to pieces. It was not something easily forgotten, and following the defeat of the Republican cause, he had returned to England a broken and disillusioned young man. So when the second great European war broke out, he wanted no part of it, registering as a conscientious objector to avoid being called up for combat, and volunteering for land work duties – a task he undertook with great resolve.

His family had long disowned him as a black sheep, though his exact legal position regarding inheritance of a title was unclear, since his father had been resident abroad for many years and was still separated, though not divorced, from his eccentric mother. The contents of the present Earl's will were not known, even to his wife. Charlie hid his true feelings behind a mask of probity and acquiescence to his fate, and was content to live a simple life of toil with his Spanish mistress in their humble surroundings. The rest of the team, except for his brother Tarquin and the Reverend Christian, respected his position and admired him for his principles and the sacrifices he had made, though they were members of a lower class and background.

Charlie took his guard at the wicket, exuding a false air of calm and confidence. Forty yards away, young Michael Mellors was scratching out his mark to begin his run up to bowl. He was a tall, gangly though muscular youth, with thick blond hair and rippling muscles, and the look of a man on a mission. The Commodore took his time organising the field, which only added to the batsman's tension; three slips and two gullies, the wider of which was Cedric himself. The others were all posted close to the wicket – intimidatingly close. Only Reg, ignominiously assigned to long leg, protected the boundary.

After what seemed an eternity to Charlie, Mellors came steaming in to bowl the first ball, puffing and panting like a runaway train, arms and legs flailing, disconcertingly delivering the ball off the wrong foot, which made it awkward for the batsman to pick up in flight. Charlie barely had time to move as the ball whistled past his nose and thudded into Archie Duncan's gloves.

'No ball!' yelled Ken, Mellors having overstepped the bowling crease by almost a foot.

The next delivery was of identical length, except that this time it hit an undulation in the deteriorating pitch and skidded through low, striking the batsman a painful blow on the instep. Cursing the fact that he still had to face another five balls, Charlie settled down in his block again. The next ball reared and struck him painfully in the chest.

'Sorry, batsman,' said Mellors, retrieving the ball.

'No harm done,' winced Charlie.

'You alright, old boy?' enquired the Commodore.

Alf wandered down the pitch to say something, but Charlie waved him away, though his ribs hurt like hell.

The next delivery was even faster, and Charlie was like a rabbit caught in the headlights, unable to move, and barely saw the ball as it whistled past him. Archie fumbled it this time, and the batsmen could have run for a bye. Alf advanced a few yards down the pitch, then thought better of it, spluttering, 'Yes... sorry... no... sorry, Charlie, stay there!'

Back outside the pavilion, the rest of the Rotting Hillers were watching with some apprehension.

'He shouldn't be allowed to play in this sort of game,' moaned Ted. 'He'll kill someone at this rate!'

'Oh God, he's funking it,' cried Tarquin in his upper-class whine, somewhere between pathos and sarcasm. 'His nerve's gone. He's been like this ever since getting bombed in Barcelona. The poor man's a wreck.' Tarquin spoke as if mocking his brother, though doubtless he would have performed no better against the local speed merchant.

'If he's bowling, I'm definitely not batting,' groaned Ted, exaggerating a limp as he went to sit down.

Two deliveries later, the ball finally made contact with Charlie's bat, as a tentative prod resulted in a gentle glance down the leg side, though the ball did not run very far. 'Yes, come on!' screamed Charlie, though it was not his call, and his partner would be running to the danger end.

'Blinkin' flip, Charlie!' cried Alf, realising too late that his partner had already run halfway down the pitch.

Instinctively, the old man began to run, his little legs shuffling as fast as they could, but it was a hopeless cause. Barely had he set off and passed Charlie in no man's land, than the athletic young Derek Melville swooped in from square leg and hurled the return into Archie's gloves, who whipped off the bails with a loud cry of triumph. Alf cursed, then tucked his bat under his arm and marched hurriedly off, not looking at his captain, his face crimson and breathless.

Charlie stood crestfallen at the other end, leaning on his bat. 'I really am so sorry, Alf. I know how irritating it can be.'

Alf did not acknowledge him. Irritating was not the word. Poor 'Lucky' had been run out without facing a ball!

'That's a good start,' cooed Daphne, back at the scorers' table.

Hazel sniffed and said nothing, then advised her colleague of the next batsman, the Reverend Christian, giving her usual thumbnail sketch.

'That's a good name for a man of the church – Christian,' commented Daphne, trying to make polite conversation.

''E's descended from that bloke in *Mutiny on the Bounty*,' advised Hazel.

'I beg your pardon?'

'Y' know, Clark Gable.'

'What are you talking about?'

'Y'know – "Mutiny, Mr. Christian. Mutiny!' bellowed Hazel, rendering a surprisingly accurate rendition of the actor Charles Laughton.

For a moment, Daphne stared at Hazel, open-mouthed in astonishment, then resumed her business, writing the vicar's name in her scorebook. 'Fletcher Christian,' added Hazel. 'That was the geezer's name, wannit?'

'Oh really,' sniffed Daphne, 'how interesting.' Then, like a light bulb flickering on, a question entered her mind. 'But I thought those mutineers ended up on some island in the middle of nowhere and were never heard of again. So how can your man be descended from him?'

'I dunno. I didn't write the film, did I? Must've all 'appened before he went to sea.'

Daphne shook her head and admitted defeat, not realising Hazel was winding her up.

Micky's father, Gilbert Mellors, opened the bowling from the other end. He was military medium pace, far less intimidating but naggingly accurate. Still rooted to the crease, Charlie played out a maiden over with little incident. The vicar then edged the first ball of Micky Mellors' next over through the slips, diplomatically declining to take a second run. Somehow, the pair survived the onslaught for the next few minutes before

Charlie, finally losing his nerve completely and edging backwards to the leg side, exposed his wicket to the fast bowler and saw his stumps splayed in all directions. Mellors came galloping down the pitch, letting out a huge roar of triumph.

'Hard cheese, old boy,' commiserated Cedric, as Charlie loped disconsolately away.

'Ooh, seven for two wickets then,' purred Daphne gleefully.

Back outside the pavilion, Wally was getting ever more windy, due in fourth wicket down. Hazel gave him a knowing glance. 'Better get padded up, luv,' she said, as Tarquin lolloped out to replace his fallen brother.

'I don't like the look of this,' Wally muttered to Billy.

'Put me in next. I'll give them some stick,' suggested Billy, as Charlie mooched past.

'Don't be silly, you wouldn't last two balls,' sighed his captain, flopping down in the nearest deckchair and unbuckling his pads.

'It's not fair,' griped Ted. 'I told you, he shouldn't be allowed to play in this game.'

As if to contradict this, young Mellors sent down a long hop, which the Reverend pulled away to mid-wicket for a massive six, going down on one knee and holding a dramatic pose for several seconds.

'I wish he wouldn't show off like that,' implored Charlie.

'What's the betting he's out next ball? 'suggested Wally.

All too predictably, Chris tried to repeat the same shot to the next delivery, which was quicker and more pitched up. Cramped for room, he got a top edge on the bat, the ball sailing high in a loop to square leg, where Jimmy Catt pouched a straightforward catch. The vicar lurched from the wicket, staring at his bat, then banging it violently on his pads as he cursed to heaven.

'Told you,' Wally confirmed, getting more nervous by the minute.

'Trust you to put the mockers on it!' moaned Ted.

The sad-looking scoreboard read:

Total 18 Wickets 3 Last Man 10

Tim Stewart now marched out to bat from the side of the field, cheered on madly by Fiona and Caroline, having rescued them from the attentions of 'Pussy' Catt during the tea interval and installed them back in their deckchairs on the boundary.

Wally, next man due in, now emerged from the dressing room, fully padded up, and began to pace up and down around the scorers' table. He could rarely keep still when waiting to bat next, unlike some others. Tarquin, for example, would often doze in a deckchair, and

Ted Jolly once had to be awoken from a drunken stupor, whereupon he immediately marched out to bat in completely the wrong direction and had to be guided to the wicket! Fortunately, his innings lasted just two balls on that occasion. Everyone handled it in their own way.

Wally wandered about, casually swinging his decrepit old bat at imaginary balls.

'Oh, f' gawd's sake, si'down, luv,' complained Hazel. 'Yer doin' me 'ead in!'

Wally muttered, 'Sorry,' and wandered off to stand by the scoreboard, where two young scamps were changing the numbers on Daphne's instructions.

For all his faults, Tim was a proper cricketer and knew how to bat. Early in an innings he could be very correct and circumspect. His partner Tarquin, on the other hand, did not know the meaning of caution, simply swinging his bat at every ball in a lazy, elegant manner that befitted his temperament. Left-handed like his brother, his main problem was lack of footwork: had he been able to plant his feet in the correct place, he could have been a very good batsman, but he usually looked ripe for getting out almost every ball.

Young Mellors was given a blow and Jimmy Catt was introduced into the attack, bowling a whole over of gentle seam, during which Tarquin swung his bat and missed every ball. Eventually, he finally got the measure of the bowling and began to make contact. When he did hit the ball, it tended to go a long way. He lofted one shot over mid-wicket and another high over cover point on the opposite side, though playing the same shot to both deliveries. If Tarquin had no idea where the ball was going, the fielders had even less!

Thirty runs came up, Tarquin swishing, and Tim opening up and playing some elegant drives down the ground. The 50 total was reached just as the church clock struck a quarter past six. If Rotting Hill were going to win, they needed to score another 129 in about 75 minutes, which was quite an ask. It seemed a draw would be the limit of their ambitions.

The spectators were beginning to doze in their deckchairs as the contest became almost becalmed. The Commodore now turned to the burly South African doctor, Rorke Veivers, who bowled looping, slow leg breaks. He had settled in England after the war and was something of a character in the district. Like Ken Kippax, he too suffered from the 'drift' when fielding, though in his case it usually seemed to work to his team's advantage.

Cedric would post him to some point in the field, to which he would jauntily prance with the cry of 'O.K, skep!', but then subsequently redeploy to what he believed would be a more advantageous position, which it often turned out to be. This phenomenon was humorously, though rather unimaginatively known as 'Rorke's Drift', after the famous battle with the Zulus.

In this instance, it proved the downfall of Tarquin. At the end of Veivers' first over, competently negotiated by Tim, his skipper sent him to field at cover point. But Tarquin had been slicing the ball squarer to the wicket, so as Gilbert Mellors ran in to bowl, Veivers began sidling to his right, about ten yards, and was in a perfect position as Tarquin cut the ball straight to him for a simple catch.

'Great piece of field placing, what?' chortled the Commodore, as he hobbled briskly across to congratulate the catcher.

'Ooh, needed that,' Daphne triumphed gleefully.

Back on the boundary, Walter Richardson girdled up what was left of his loins, pulled on his batting gloves, adjusted his groin protector into a more comfortable position, and meekly made his entrance onto the field.

'Good luck, Wol!' cried Hazel, but he barely heard.

Wally loved his cricket. He lived for his weekends playing or watching the game, but at this precise moment he wished he could have been anywhere else, doing anything other than what he now needed to do. He was feeling totally out of sorts; his bowels had been playing up again, and right now he felt like death warmed up. *What a strange paradox*, he philosophically mused to himself, as he wandered to the wicket, *that the very thing he loved doing the most made him feel so bad*. Hazel had told him that he would feel better once he 'got out there', but it wasn't true.

The group of fielders broke up as Wally arrived in the middle. Cedric boomed, 'Batsman in, return to your positions!' He thought he heard someone, probably Jimmy Catt, joke, 'Down to the tail now, boys!'

'Do you want a guard?' asked Alf Fortune, now having taken over the umpiring duties.

'No thanks,' mumbled the batsman, almost adding, 'I won't be staying long.'

Always a jittery starter to his innings, Wally had rarely felt more apprehensive. He fidgeted about in the crease, nervously tapping his bat on the ground as Mellors ran up to bowl. It was a straight, good length delivery, swinging slightly away. Wally prodded tentatively at the ball, which tickled the outside edge of his bat and thudded into Archie Duncan's gloves – and out again!

'Howzz… ooooh!' cried the close fielders in frustration.

Trying to appear outwardly calm, Wally walked down the pitch and prodded an imaginary spot where he thought the ball might have landed – a piece of double bluff that fooled nobody.

Back on the scorers' table, Hazel sighed in relief and lit a cigarette, much to Daphne's annoyance, as she waved her hand to blow the smoke away. 'Sorry, luv.'

As Wally faced up to the next ball, he heard somebody call out, 'Lucky bastard!' He could feel his heart thumping against the walls of his chest, aware of nothing except Archie Duncan muttering something about his own performance being 'unacceptable'.

The next two balls were wide of the wicket and Wally attempted no shot, with the final ball of the over edged towards gully, where the Commodore stopped it with his artificial limb to somewhat over-generous applause. Slowly, Wally played himself in, blocking the straight balls and leaving the wider ones. Finally, after about ten minutes, he snicked the ball between the rigid slip fielders and scampered a single, relieved to get 'off the mark'. It brought some ironic cheering from his teammates on the boundary, who were now congregated in a cluster of deckchairs to the right of the scoreboard, which now read 77 for four wickets.

By now it was almost six-thirty. The grey clouds had drifted away, and the ground was bathed in warm evening sunshine. With the batsmen playing cautiously, there was little activity on the field, with many spectators snoozing in their chairs.

Suddenly, disturbing this tranquil scene, an odd-looking figure came striding purposely around the ground, dressed in a tweed jacket and deerstalker cap. One needed to look twice to see that this tiny person was, in fact, a woman, with a time-battered, tanned face, topped with a huge pair of tortoiseshell glasses, as she hurried along with the aid of a wooden stick, apparently superfluous. As she bustled along, walking well inside the boundary rope and cutting across the corner of the outfield, a burly man, dressed entirely in a grey uniform, trailed a few yards behind her.

'Oh God!' moaned Tarquin. 'Look out, here comes Mama.'

It was indeed Lady Ashfield, accompanied by Blenkinsop, her chauffeur and general dogsbody. Puffing a little, she shuddered to a halt amidst the Rotting Hill players, and acknowledged her eldest son, who had recovered from his earlier trauma and was now relaxing in a deckchair with a cool beer and a cigarette.

'Rupert.'

'Hello, Mama.'

'Thought I'd find you here. How are you, boy?' Lady Edwina spoke briskly, like a woman on a mission with little time to accomplish it. She had a formidable reputation, and one trifled with her at their peril.

'Fair enough, thanks,' replied Charlie lazily.

'Good, call up at the Manor sometime. I need to discuss something with you. Had a letter from your father.'

'Yes, Mama.'

'And for God's sake, smarten yourself up, boy. You look like a bloody tramp!'

'Yes, Mama.'

'Ah, Tarquin,' she barked, turning to her younger son. 'Seen that damn sister of yours?'

'No, Mama, I didn't know she was with you.'

'Probably fornicating in the woods with some ploughboy. Anybody seen Jolly?'

Edwina, who was distinctly short-sighted, finally spotted her head gardener asleep in a deckchair, resting his multiple injuries. 'Ah, there you are, Jolly. Knew you'd be here, lounging around as usual. Report to the house tomorrow. Got an important job for you.'

Ted, irritated at being woken from his catnap, mumbled something inaudible in reply.

'Excuse me, ma'am.' It was Alf Fortune, now relieved from his umpiring stint, who spoke up, touching the peak of his cap in reverence. 'I'm afraid Ted's badly injured. He can't walk, and his hands are black and blue keeping wicket.'

'Poppycock!' roared Her Ladyship. 'The man's a malingerer! Always has been. Jolly, report to the servants' entrance at eight o'clock sharp or there'll be hell to pay.' With that, she stomped away in the direction of the car park, closely followed by the dutiful Blenkinsop, walking straight in front of the sightscreen just as Jimmy Catt was running in to bowl. Distracted, batsman Tim Stewart quite rightly backed away, waving his bat in the direction of the miscreant.

Reg Barclay, the nearest fielder, his sense of decorum compromised by this appalling breach of cricketing etiquette, immediately launched into the offender. 'Get off the fucking pitch, you stupid bloody woman!'

Lady Edwina skidded to a halt, stiffened, then drew herself up to her full height, which was not much over five feet. 'I beg your pardon!'

'Only a halfwit would walk in front of the sightscreen when the bowling was at that end,' pointed out Reg in his best admonishing tone.

'Young man,' began Edwina, turning to face her accuser with hands on hips. 'Do you know who you are talking to?'

'I don't care if you are Her Majesty the fucking Queen, get off the sodding pitch!'

Edwina bristled even more stiffly. 'How dare you speak to me like that! Blenkinsop, take that man's name. Then go and fetch a policeman and have him arrested for using foul and abusive language in a public place. I don't know what the world's coming to. I blame the Labour Party. Winnie would never have stood for this.'

With that, she marched off, muttering to herself but not looking back. Following in her slipstream, Blenkinsop shrugged at Reg, then trudged off after his employer. The fact that the Tories had been back in power for two years had apparently escaped her attention.

After this bizarre episode, which had silenced the spectators – all except the Rotting Hill contingent, who were all laughing loudly – the game resumed once again. There had been rumours that representatives of both Surrey and Sussex County Cricket clubs were present, ostensibly to watch young Mellors, but Tim Stewart had got wind of it and was playing an innings of classical caution; in fact, he was showing more responsibility on the cricket field than he had ever done in his entire life outside it. At the other end, Wally, having grown in confidence and feeling a little more himself, had begun to push, glance, and nurdle the odd single. The score crept up slowly. Several mid-pitch conferences between the batsmen had discussed 'playing for the draw', and with less than an hour to play, this now looked the most likely result.

Following Lady Edwina's departure, calm descended once again upon West Rotting cricket ground. The game had fallen into a lull, with neither batsmen nor bowlers showing much regard to changing the course of the contest. It seemed that, barring something unforeseeable, the day would end with honours even. Players and spectators alike began to sense this, and a pastoral tranquillity now spread over proceedings.

'Looks like they're shutting up shop,' observed the Colonel from beneath the big oak tree.

Jack Hurst didn't reply; he had dozed off.

Chapter Fourteen

August 23rd 6.40pm

BARRY

Whilst most of his team were now sitting down, Billy Moon was padded up, ready to bat, standing rather oddly and grimacing, with his hand down his flannels, fiddling with his 'box'.

'What's up with you, Bill, feelin' a bit fruity?' joked Alf.

Billy had been staring at the two women at the scorers' table for some time, and replied, 'Cor, she don'alf give me the 'orn!'

'Who?' queried Ted, barely recovered from his confrontation with Lady Edwina. 'You mean Hazel?'

'No,' Billy shifted his weight awkwardly from one leg to the other, 'the well-stacked piece in the orange dress.'

'What, you don't mean ol' Daphne?' laughed Alf. 'Blinkin' flip, Bill, you must be gettin' desperate!'

'Everyone gives Billy the horn,' observed Tarquin drily.

'He's not wankin' off again, is he?' joked Ken.

'Yeah,' chimed in Barry, also padded up and playing air shots with his bat. 'Even Ted gives Billy the 'orn.'

Ted ignored him but instead commented, 'Funny, isn't it, how all the scorers these days seem to be fat, middle-aged women?'

'Perhaps you should take it up then,' chortled Barry.

Ted finally rose to the bait. 'Yes, Barry, and they've got a tax inspector in their team. I'm sure he'd be more than interested in some of your activities.'

Barry giggled. Tired of needling Ted, he wandered away looking for someone to give him a knock-up, with a parting shot, 'And don't forget that important job you've got for Her Ladyship. Better borrow some rubber johnnies off Tim.'

'Dad, what's wanking off?' asked a curious Ivan Kippax.

'Sex without the nagging, son,' replied his father philosophically. The boy wandered away looking none the wiser.

'Why don't you ask 'er for a bit then?' Alf said to Billy, nodding in the direction of the scorers.

'Don't tell Hazel, though,' grinned Tarquin.

'Hang on, isn't she the Commodore's bit of crumpet?' said Charlie.

'Eh?' queried Billy, totally puzzled by the conversation.

'Yeah, Billy loves knobbing the scorers,' laughed Ken. 'He thinks they'll give him some extra runs.'

Everyone laughed out loud as the ribald banter continued between Alf and Ken, mostly at Billy's expense.

'Cedric told me she likes to take it up the chuff.'

'Eh?'

'Takes it up the what?'

'Does 'e do it with 'is leg on or off?'

'Eh?'

'Has Billy got the 'orn again?'

'Wake up!'

'I'd run it under a cold tap if I were you, Bill. You don't want it getting' in the way when you're battin'!'

'Eh?'

'Don't confuse 'im.'

'She's a bit out of your league, ain't she, Bill?'

'Naah, them fat bints go like bunnies.'

'How do you know that then, Alf?'

'Well, I was in Italy during the war, wanni?'

'What's that got to do with anything?'

'Gentlemen, please!' interrupted the Reverend Christian, who had been chatting nearby to the wife of one of the West Rotting players. 'Kindly temper your language, there are ladies present.'

'Where?'

'You know,' added Tarquin, drifting off on another tack entirely, 'I think Barry may be a latent homosexual.'

'A late what?' asked Billy. There came no answer, for just at that moment a loud roar came from the middle of the pitch.

'Where's Barry? You're in,' called out Alf.

With the match drifting into nothingness, the Commodore had belatedly unleashed his vast knowledge of tactical perspicacity. He may not have been much of a contributor with the bat and ball any more, but he still had a cute cricketing brain that more than justified his presence on the field. With the batsmen seemingly well settled, he began to switch his bowlers and fielders around, bringing back Veivers for one over, swopping Pussy Catt for Dan Sweeney, West Rotting's Tory councillor, then played his trump card by bringing on Micky Mellors for a quick burst. It did the trick: with the last ball of his comeback over, the fast bowler sneaked one through Tim's defences, which up until then had been exemplary, bringing back an inswinger to clip the top of the off stump.

As Barrimore Garibaldi Dick strode purposefully to the wicket, Wally walked out to greet him. 'We're still 90 short,' he pointed out. 'There's only three-quarters of an hour left. With a bit of luck, we can hold out for a draw.'

Barry took no notice. 'Let's liven this game up,' he commanded.

Barry survived the last ball of Mellors' over, allowing it to hit him in the ribs. He might be considered a pain in the backside, but he had an impish approach to the game that defied any natural logic. Neither did he lack physical courage, being broad-shouldered and powerful in his upper body. His thick, black hair was tied in a small knot at the back of his neck, which emphasised his swarthy, gypsy-like appearance.

The first ball of the next over, bowled by Dan Sweeney, was glanced away by Wally for a single, bringing Barry back on strike. After a couple of heaves at the ball – one which he missed entirely, and the other deflected onto his pads – Barry finally made contact, flat batting the ball to the boundary with tremendous velocity. Sweeney's next delivery met the same fate, as did the one after that (called a no-ball by the new umpire Charlie – the reason for which, he later confessed, 'because he's a bloody Tory!') was top-edged over the wicket keeper, just failing to reach the boundary, the batsmen running three. Caught up in the mood, Wally deftly cut the extra ball through the covers for an easy two.

Jimmy Catt was then brought on to bowl, replacing Mellors, and with his first ball had Barry caught behind the wicket, stretching for a wide ball.

It had been an exciting, if brief cameo by the outgoing batsman, but it had suddenly changed the nature of the match. Spectators, many of whom had seemingly lost interest in the contest, began to sit up and take notice. Under the oak tree, even Jack Hurst had woken up, especially as Billy Moon now stumbled awkwardly out to bat, still fiddling with his box, which didn't appear to fit properly into his underpants.

Jack lit his pipe. 'This could be interestin', big fella's comin' in.'

'Won't last an over,' stated the Colonel. 'The man's just a slogger, no technique at all. Pitch one up and you'll do him.'

'Aye, we'll see,' muttered Jack. 'We'll see.'

Back at the scorers' table, Daphne noted the name of the new batsman. 'Isn't he your boyfriend?' she said to Hazel, smirking. Hazel gave her a withering look and said nothing, but wondered, *What does she know about that?*

Billy reached the crease and immediately settled into his position to receive his first ball, not bothering with a guard, and crouching across the wicket with his feet well apart and outside the line of the stumps. It was a distinctly ungainly stance, not to be found in any coaching manual, reminding Jack of the great hitter Gilbert Jessop, whose century had famously won a Test match for England against Australia.

'Bowl at his legs,' Cedric instructed the bowler. Jimmy did that, at least for a couple of balls, and it seemed to work, as Billy could not adjust his static position to free his arms. Cramped for room, he could only pat the ball away on the leg side. But Jimmy was too conventional a cricketer to bowl defensively in that manner, and the very next ball was straight and on a good length. Billy opened his shoulders, and the ball screamed away off his broad bat to the offside boundary, scattering a gaggle of children playing there.

'Hey, watch out!' cried a nearby spectator.

Two deliveries later, the same thing happened. When Billy got to the other end, Dan Sweeney received the same treatment. Billy simply splayed his legs and teed off. Most days he would have only lasted a few balls before getting out, but on this day, his luck was in. Sometimes the ball sailed in the air, just eluding the fielders; sometimes it caught an awkward part of his bat and edged away for another four. But in no time, he had accumulated 20 runs.

Cedric was forced to bring back Micky Mellors for a final burst, but Billy treated his bowling just the same. A loud murmur passed around the ground, as everyone now began to take notice of what was happening. Billy clumped Sweeney's opening delivery of another over hard in the direction of mid-off, currently patrolled by Reg Barclay. With a nimble skip and jump, he hopped out of the way of the rocketing sphere, which crashed into the boundary, causing some of the Rotting Hill contingent to move smartly out of the way, accompanied by hearty cheering.

It was the quickest Reg had moved all day and brought a stinging rebuke from his captain. 'You bumsucking bogeybucket! You're there to stop the bloody ball, not get out of the way!'

'As if you would have stopped it,' smarted Reg under his breath, retrieving the ball from the leering Rotting Hillers.

Two balls later, Billy smashed another delivery straight back at the bowler, almost decapitating him and umpire Charlie. The next one went sailing over mid-wicket for six, a trajectory so low that fielder Dan Sweeney had to duck out of the way rather than try to catch it, before bouncing into the side of the tennis courts, just missing Fiona and Caroline, cuddling with Tim on one of the wooden benches.

'Oi, Moon, watch it! You almost took out me totty!' Tim yelled, pulling a giggling Fiona closer to him.

'Isn't this exciting?' hooted Caroline.

'Mmm, ya,' bubbled Fiona.

'Catch it, you piddling poopbucket!' bawled the Commodore, now getting red in the face, steam coming out of his ears. 'Go and stand by the boundary!'

Dinsdale Aubrey Norton Sweeney ('Dan' to his acquaintances) had never been the greatest fielder, due to his inbred fear of being hit by the ball. He was something of a celebrity in the district; a failed politician, he had ruined his chances of becoming the local Conservative Member of Parliament after a notorious and much-publicised affair with the wife of the constituency party chairman. Worse still, whilst a member of the local council, several lucrative contracts had mysteriously gone the way of his building business, which had subsequently gone bankrupt. He still, however, remained president of the nearby Hurst Park Golf Club, where he was allowed to cheat unmercifully – it was a standing joke among the members that when Dan hit a wayward shot, he shouted not 'fore!' but 'three!'. Notwithstanding all this, he remained a personable chap, engaging in a roguish kind of way, and was popular with the cricket fraternity, especially the ladies, as a useful if somewhat erratic cricketer, who once claimed to have played for Surrey second eleven.

The next ball from Mellors was shorter and bounced higher, and hooked in the same direction by Billy, but the ball made contact with the top of his bat and looped higher and higher as it spiralled towards the mid-wicket boundary, to where Dan Sweeney had been re-positioned. The fielder came running in, arms flailing wildly, threw down his cap onto the ground, and watched as the ball sailed over his head, before pitching once and dribbling over the boundary.

'Sorry, skip, sun in my eyes,' Dan explained, ignoring the fact that it was setting behind him and had just disappeared behind a cloud.

The Commodore exploded,' You todgering tossbucket! You piss-stained pile of number twos! Go to cover point and change places with Jimmy.'

And so it continued; no matter which bowler was tried, Billy treated them all with the same disdain. Wally was content to nudge the odd single and let his partner take the bowling. The spectators were now all fully attentive and carefully watching the scenario now playing out before them, if only to stay alert as five-and-a-quarter ounces of solid cork and leather began hurtling around the ground in all directions. The small knot of Rotting Hill players and supporters were applauding every hit wildly. Behind the stumps, Archie Duncan was griping in true wicket-keeper fashion; the bowling being 'totally unacceptable' and the fielding 'completely unacceptable'.

'Pitch the bloody ball up!' barked Cedric.

'Bowl it straighter,' snarled Archie.

The score was now increasing so rapidly that the two small boys changing the tins on the scoreboard could not keep up, and badgered Daphne incessantly for the correct score. Hazel, grinning like a Cheshire cat, was scribbling furiously in her own scorebook as her colleague became more and more testy. Cedric was now changing the bowlers so often that Daphne got into a muddle with her coloured pencils. Eventually, the point of one of them splintered as she was writing.

'Oh, buggering bumholes!' she cursed loudly.

'Steady on. Language, dear,' rebuked her colleague, 'there's kiddies about. That's another four, by the way. Need any 'elp?'

'Yes, I'm quite aware of that, excuse me. No thank you very much!' grumbled Daphne, frantically sharpening her broken pencil.

'Keep up then, dear.'

'Ohhhh!'

Eventually, during a brief break as Billy took a drink, the boys correctly updated the board to:

Total 145 Wickets 6 Last Man 11

After each blow to his bowling, not to mention his young ego, Mellors followed through almost the whole way down the pitch and glared at Billy, hands on hips, cursing loudly, as the batsman ignored him, rubbing his nose, clearing his throat, and adjusting his abdominal protector. Wally's nurdled and scampered singles proved almost as irritating to the fielding side, who were now in complete disarray and meltdown.

After another expensive over ended, the Commodore stood in the middle of the pitch, pulled off his harlequin cap, and began to furiously scratch his bald dome. The amiable Rorke Veivers sidled up to him, his jolly face bathed in a broad grin. 'Lut me hev a gur at hem, skip,' he drawled in his thick Cape Town accent. 'Arl gut hem art. He buts lek a bluddy kaffir!'

With no other options working, Cedric reluctantly tossed him the ball. Wally noted the big South African limbering up as he trotted down the wicket to talk to Billy. He knew his partner could bash fast or medium-paced bowling all over the park if his luck was in, but he was all at sea against the spinners.

'Look, Bill, we've almost got them licked. They're all over the place. We only need about another 25. Watch out for this bloke. Wait for the bad ball and whack it. Don't do anything silly.'

'Right,' nodded a panting Billy. 'Right you are.'

But Wally knew he was wasting his breath. Billy was impervious to any advice; he simply played by instinct. Veivers' first ball was deliberately tossed up high, and Billy's eyes widened as he watched it floating gently towards him, lurching wildly down the pitch to have a huge heave at the ball, head in the air. It pitched just in front of him, spun away from the bat, then in and out of Archie Duncan's gloves, as the big man swivelled violently to regain his ground just in time before the 'keeper could gather the ball cleanly.

Desperately, Wally ran down the pitch to offer more advice. 'Take it easy, Bill. Wait for the loose one. Remember, there's only Rag, Tag, and Bobtail to come in after you.'

'More like Andy Pandy, and Bill and Ben.'

Somewhat surprised at his partner's in-depth knowledge of children's television programmes, Wally wandered back slowly to the non-striker's end. It was no use; he could see it coming a mile off. The next ball was tossed even higher, and Billy's eyes widened even further. He stumbled down the wicket, aimed a tremendous blow, and missed the ball by yards. This time the wicket keeper made no mistake, taking the ball cleanly and whipping off the bails in one co-ordinated movement. Billy swung round and threw himself, bat first, at the crease, even then landing two feet short in an undignified heap, to see the wicket shattered behind him.

The Rotting Hill team greeted this with a mixture of hilarity and disappointment.

'Dickhead!' shouted Ken.

'What a twerp,' added Alf.

Billy slowly and painfully picked himself up, covered in dust and earth, a huge grin all over his red face, and returned to his teammates to loud applause from all round the ground. 'Sorry, lads,' he commented, 'just lost my constipation for a minute. Got caught in two-man's land.'

Ken Kippax walked briskly out to replace him, throwing away a cigarette. Wally knew Ken was a limited batsman. He could bravely defend his wicket if needs be, but his attacking strokes were restricted to a leg-side mow, eyes shut, and preferably to a high, slow full toss. The only reason he batted higher than Ted Jolly was entirely due to the latter's total lack of self-esteem.

Somehow, Ken survived the rest of the over, even getting two runs miscuing a full toss. It was now almost a quarter past seven; there would still be time for four, possibly five more overs before 'stumps' were called to signal the end of the match. Twenty-two runs were still required for a win, with three wickets in hand. Wally knew it was down to him if Rotting Hill were to win or draw the game. A mid-pitch conference with Ken failed to agree upon tactics; Wally still opting for the draw, but Ken gung-ho for a win. Whatever was to happen, Wally knew he must try and farm the bowling and keep the less capable batsmen away from the strike.

His heart sank as he noted Micky Mellors being thrown the ball.

Back at the scorers' table, Hazel lit another cigarette.

Chapter Fifteen

August 23rd 7.15pm

TED

Bing, bing, bing, bong! chimed the quarter hour on the Christ Church clock, causing Wally to step away from the wicket, just as Mellors was steaming in to deliver the ball. *That'll waste a few more seconds*, thought Wally. Conversely though, it would make the young fast bowler a little angrier. In an attempt to diffuse the situation, Wally wandered down the pitch doing a spot of gardening, first with his bat, then with his glove, brushing some loose bits off earth away.

'Cam on, mun, git on with et!' complained Veivers, now positioned at forward short leg, only yards from the bat. Only when Wally walked back to the crease did he notice how close the field had been brought in.

Mellors came pounding in once more, blowing and panting, arms flailing. 'Get behind the line,' Wally muttered under his breath. 'Get behind the line.' The ball whipped down, skidded, then caught the edge of Wally's old bat, squirting away between the Commodore in the gully and the roly-poly Peregrine Hacker, a few yards to his left at slip. Two less agile fielders it was hard to imagine. As they both stared at each other, neither wishing to run after the ball for obvious physical reasons, Wally sensed an opportunity.

'Come on, Ken, two-it!' he yelled. The batsmen crossed for two runs easily, as Pussy Catt had to scamper round from cover point to retrieve the ball. The rest of the over was unplayable, Mellors having worked himself up into a frenzy, bowling faster than ever on the deteriorating turf. Wally frantically shuffled across his wicket for each delivery, bat to the front, pads and body behind, but all bar one ball fizzed wide of the off stump. The other thudded into his pads, juddering his knee, but umpire Charlie immediately called 'no ball' and started to nonchalantly examine what was left of the bowling crease with his boot.

'Shit!' cursed Mellors, aiming a kick at nothing in particular. Desperately, Wally tried to manufacture a single from the last ball of the over to keep the strike away from Ken, but all he saw was a red blur whistling past his nose. As the field changed around for the next over, Wally glanced at the updated scoreboard, which now read:

Total 160 Wickets 7 Last Man 46

Ken Kippax was hopping about nervously in his crease, like a cat on hot coals. Wally perceived him eyeing the leg side boundary as Veivers pranced in to bowl. Wally shut his eyes, for he guessed what was coming. The spinner held the ball back slightly, Ken turned his head, swung his bat horizontally across the line, failed to make contact and was struck on his back leg right in front of the stumps.

'Howzettt!' screamed the bowler, straight in the umpire's face. Up went the finger in agreement and off marched Ken as if he were on the parade ground, accompanied by an audible groan from the boundary and a giggle of glee from Daphne.

Only Ted and Ken's boy Ivan now remained of the batters. Having moaned all day about his injuries and not wanting to bat, Ted was bullied and shamed into going in next. He strode briskly out to the middle, at least for the first few paces, before remembering his injured ankle, hobbling the last few yards to the wicket.

There's still a chance, thought Wally. Ted's one shot was a cross bat mow, usually hit in an arc between backward square leg and forward square leg, but against the slower bowlers he sometimes got in right and had been a very occasional match winner on his day. Veivers' first two deliveries spun slowly away from the bat, missing Ted's mechanical pull shot by yards, but the next met the middle of the bat perfectly and was heaved away just wide of the square leg fielder for four runs. The next ball, Ted repeated the shot, with the same result, the ball going slightly the other side of the same fielder. His teammates hooted like mad as Cedric hopped up and down in frustration, cursing loudly. Eight more runs!

On the mid-wicket boundary, Fiona and Caroline, now accompanied by both Tim and Tarquin, screamed wildly and danced up and down, crying, 'Rotting Hill, Rotting Hill, ya, ya, ya!'

The last two balls of the over rapped Ted on the pads as he tried to repeat the shot and missed, both raucous appeals turned down by the umpire – both pitching outside the leg stump – as the fielders leapt about in the excitement.

Wally glanced at the clock on the church tower, now showing 25 past seven. The evening was slowly drawing in, though the light was still good. There was time for two more overs, possibly only one if it was bowled by young Mellors, which it almost certainly would be. With a spot of gamesmanship, Wally could surely drag it out for five more minutes.

The batsmen met in the middle for a brief conference as the field changed over. 'Let's go for it!' snapped Ted with his newly-found bravado, turning away before Wally could reply.

To save time, Mellors shortened his run-up, but with no appreciable loss of pace. His first ball nipped back off the pitch, straight for Wally's midriff. Jumping in the air, he fended it away with the face of his bat off his hip down to fine leg, where Reg Barclay had now been stationed. The ball was hurrying swiftly through the bumpy outfield, but Reg looked favourite to get to it before it crossed the boundary.

'Come on, Reg, get it in!' yelled the Commodore, as the batsmen completed one run and turned for another.

Reg bent down stiffly to grasp the ball, body right behind, but just in the instant before reaching him, it hit a bump in the turf, hopped up, and slipped first through his arms, then between his legs, and dribbled over the boundary rope for four more runs, met with some ironic cheering from the direction of the scoreboard.

The Commodore's blood pressure finally reached boiling point. 'You ovulating cuntbucket!' he shrieked. 'Wake up, you blithering bumbollock.'

Back at the table, Hazel stood up and cheered to the rafters; Daphne sitting tight-lipped. 'Sit down, please,' she commanded stiffly.

Fuming, Reg vented his anger on the barrackers, throwing a stiff reverse Churchillian salute in their direction, which was met with a collection of catcalls.

Flushed with success, Wally drove the next ball – a juicy half volley – back past the bowler but straight to the fielder at mid-off, making a funny sound on his bat. He glanced down at it and saw a split developing around the splice at the top. *Too late to change it now*, he thought. The next ball was ultra-fast, spat off the crumbling turf, catching the top of Wally's bat and looping gently up into the air. For a brief second nobody moved, then everyone suddenly realised it was going to fall directly to Cedric in the gully position.

'Yours, skipper!' cried Neville Dodds from the slips. For a moment, Cedric seemed to be oblivious to what was happening, then suddenly realised that the ball was dropping straight into his hands; he did not even have to move. Unfortunately for him, young Derek Melville, fielding a few yards away, had also been watching the ball. The lad was fit and keen as mustard, winning many plaudits for his athleticism around the field saving runs. Derek only had eyes for the ball and did not seem to realise his captain was there. The cherry plopped safely into Cedric's cupped hands a split second before his world turned upside down. The two fielders collided with a sickening thud, both crashing to the ground in pain, the ball popping out harmlessly onto the ground.

'Yessss!' bellowed Ted, galloping down the pitch, his injured ankle now miraculously healed.

'Noooo!' screamed Wally, holding up his hand.

'Come on! Go on!' hollered Ted, now almost on top of his partner.

Wally had no choice, scampering off to the other end of the pitch. He saw the ball fizz past him, but it was fired in so hard that the fielder at the bowler's end could not gather it cleanly, and Wally made his ground. Turning, he tried to remonstrate with Ted, but had no breath to spare. Ted was not listening anywhere, suddenly remembering his injured ankle.

The rest of the fielders hurried to the aid of the stricken men. Cedric would be unable to regain his feet unaided, so Neville Dodds put his hands under the Commodore's armpits and hauled him upright. Sadly, young Melville had come off far worse in the collision, and was cowering on his knees, grasping his injured shoulder and neck, waiting for the storm to break.

Cedric dusted himself down, then let rip. 'You blithering, blind, blundering, bumbuggering bilgebowl, didn't you see me there!' Melville mumbled a feeble apology and slunk painfully back to his position, still grasping his injured shoulder.

Back on the boundary, the Rotting Hill players were in hysterics, particularly Billy Moon, who was rolling around on the floor laughing. Hazel was desperately trying to keep a straight face as Daphne gazed crestfallen at her hero. Even umpire Charlie found it impossible to suppress a huge grin as he enquired, 'Everyone all right?'

When play resumed, Mellors hurtled in off his short run and let rip a fearsome yorker which Ted, backing away frantically to the leg side, never saw until it demolished his wicket, sending stumps and bails flying in all directions. The bowler bounded down the pitch, whooping and hollering. For a moment, Ted stood still, looking as if he was just about to brain Mellors with his bat, then thought better of it, turned and limped off, head down, muttering all the way.

As young Ivan Kippax gingerly made his way out to the middle, his big bat trailing awkwardly behind him, Wally quickly glanced at the clock, then at the scoreboard as the young scamps hurriedly updated it. He leaned nonchalantly on his bat, seemingly without a care in the world. 'Take your time, son,' he murmured.

Like a father leading his offspring out for a swim in the sea for the first time, Ken had followed his boy out onto the field for a while, then sent him on his way with a slap on the back. Feeling he must do something, Wally met the lad as he timidly reached the wicket, looking terrified and bewildered as the fielders clapped him in and then dispersed to their positions.

'Don't worry, son, he's not as quick as he looks. Just block it. Only three balls to face.' Wally was waffling and he knew it. There just might be time for one more over. If there was, he would have to face it. The boy must hang in there somehow or steal a run from the next ball. That didn't seem very likely as Ivan took strike and faced the bowler, looking frail and tiny as the fielders closed in around him, both his bat and pads too big for him.

'What shall I do, skip?' enquired Mellors.

'Burl luk ya alwess do,' requested the ruthless Veivers. Cedric nodded.

Mellors loped in slowly off an even shorter run, with no appreciable loss of pace. The ball spat off the pitch, with Ivan transfixed like a rabbit in the headlights as it whistled past his head. Back by the scoreboard, Ken lit yet another cigarette and began to wander aimlessly around like an expectant father. 'If he hurts my boy,' he cussed, 'I'll wrap my fuckin' bat round 'is 'ead!'

The tension was now almost unbearable as the surreal scene acted out before the enthralled audience. The next ball fizzed through, well-pitched up and dead-on target, but Ivan, backing away, just got enough bat down to prevent it hitting the stumps as the crowd gasped. Ken could hardly bear to watch. Wally stood transfixed at the other end, powerless to influence events.

Twenty-nine minutes past seven – one ball left in the over. Mellors hurriedly turned and bounded in again; the ball hit a soft spot on the wicket and shot straight along the ground, passing both the stumps and the wicket-keeper's despairing dive.

'Run!' screeched Wally. 'Run, run, run!'

The ball zipped along the ground, seemingly heading for the sightscreen, but this time Reg, his feathers ruffled, was onto it like a flash. Determined not to be made to look a fool again, he flogged his plump frame around the boundary for all it was worth and hurled himself at the ball, bellyflopping like a beached whale. It was totally comical and highly undignified, but it did the trick, the ball bouncing off his paunch as he lay on the ground. Quickly picking himself up, he hurled the ball back towards the wicket with a girly-like throw. It bounced four times and went nowhere the 'keeper, but the batsmen had run two byes and stopped.

Wally knew he must keep the strike if there was to be another over. As Cedric led the applause for Reg's efforts, Wally was barracked by his own teammates for not attempting a third run.

'Shut up, you lot!' admonished Hazel. 'Wally knows what 'e's doin.' They all piped down.

The ground hushed to await the umpire's decision as to whether another over could be bowled. The fielders hurriedly changed around. Jimmy Catt was thrown the ball. The umpires moved to their positions, Charlie at the bowler's end and Victor Putney, West Rotting's non-playing arbiter, at square leg. Charlie reached his post just before the clock struck half-past seven.

'Last over then, gentlemen,' he announced in his drole but authoritative voice. Putney nodded in agreement.

'Bing, bing, bong, bing: bong, bong, bing, bong,' chimed the church tower. The ground hushed as the reliable Jimmy Catt chugged in to deliver the final over of the game.

Six balls were left to bowl and four results were still possible: Rotting Hill needed four runs to win; West Rotting needed to take one more wicket. It could be a draw, with no team winning, or even a tie with the scores level and both innings completed.

Wally suddenly realised he was on his own. He gazed at the other end for some succour, but Charlie's face was impassive and young Ivan looked totally bemused. Wally knew it was down to him. If Rotting Hill were to save the game, it would be down to him. If they won the match, it would be down to him. Worse still, if they now lost the game, it would be his fault. The whole weight of the world was on his shoulders – it was too much. He felt all humanity was now focused on him. He felt his legs wobbling, his stomach churning; inside his thick, old batting gloves, his hands were soaking wet. Desperately, he tried to focus on something. He thought of Hazel.

Jimmy ran in and let go the first ball. It was straight, just short of a length, and Wally could only block it. He glanced around the field, cannily placed by the experienced West Rotting captain: there was a man deep on the off side, another on the leg side; fine leg was almost a long stop, all three protecting the boundary. The inner field was set deep, allowing Wally a single if he wanted it, but he knew that could not be risked. He must score two 2s or a four. *If he was his namesake Wally Hammond*, he thought, *he would execute a perfect cover drive*. The great Bradman would jump down the wicket and drive or pull the ball for four with no apparent effort. If he were his great hero Denis Compton, he would improvise a flashing stroke from nowhere to astonish the fielders.

But he was none of these people, and he knew it. He was just plain old Walter George Richardson – village cricketer – and past his best at that. His whole life seemed to flash before his eyes as Jimmy ran in again, the crowd hushed and expectant. This time a quicker ball, angling away to the off side. Wally groped forward and fenced at it, missing the ball by a fraction as it thudded into Archie's gloves. The close fielders hissed in frustration, throwing their arms skywards. Back by the scoreboard, nobody moved. Hazel felt her heart thumping inside her breast. 'Lucky bastard!' someone cried from behind the wicket.

'Great bowling, Pussy,' chirped Cedric, clapping his hands, now recovered from his earlier humiliation.

Wally took guard once more, feeling his arms and legs turning to jelly, and wishing he was anywhere but there. Instinctively, all the fielders, sensing victory, moved in a few yards, as if all drawn by an imaginary magnet. All went silent once more, except for the sound of a sheep bleating in a nearby field. Jimmy bowled again, this time swinging the ball inwards towards Wally's pads. It was a fuller length, and the batsman just jammed his bat down in time to get a nick before thudding into his legs.

'Howzattt!' yelled every fielder in unison. Everyone held their breath.

'Not out,' said Charlie calmly. 'Inside edge.'

The ball had squirted away into a space. Everyone in the Rotting Hill party screamed, 'Run!' Startled, Ivan Kippax sprung from his crease.

'Noooo!' shrieked Wally, holding up a hand.

The Rotting Hillers stamped about in frustration. 'What's 'e playin' at?' beseeched Billy. 'There was an easy run there!'

'He's keepin' the boy away from the bowling,' explained Ken, now fidgeting about like a wet hen.

Hazel could stand it no more. She entered a dot in the bowler's analysis, then put down her pencil, stood up, and bummed another cigarette off Ken.

'Come on, Jimmy,' pleaded Daphne, 'you can do it.'

'Come on, Wally,' whispered Hazel.

The field was brought in even closer, claustrophobically tightening the net around Wally – not helped by the fact that the two men closest to him, Rorke Veivers and Peregrine Hacker, cast giant oval shadows over the pitch. Even the deep fielders were brought in, with only the long stop behind the wicket keeper remaining on the boundary.

Wally felt extremely hot, as if he were about to faint. His mind drifted away, and suddenly there was Denis Compton, sidling up to him, dressed in his scruffy white shirt and pads, greased hair slicked back, and bat tucked under his arm in familiar pose. 'What's up, old boy, getting a bit windy?'

'I can't do it, Denis,' Wally bleated. 'I'm going to let everyone down, it's not fair. I can't take the responsibility.' As he spoke, the fielders seemed to drift hazily around them, as if they were not part of this scene, but belonged instead to another time and dimension.

'Now look here, old chap,' said Denis, putting a comforting hand on Wally's shoulder, 'just relax. Cricket's only a game, after all is said and done. It's there to be enjoyed. Take a deep breath and do what comes naturally to you. OK, old boy?'

Then suddenly the sounds around Wally grew louder. He could hear the fielders talking amongst themselves as Cedric organized yet another minute field change.

Denis was gone; instead, he saw young Ivan Kippax standing before him.

'You alright, Mister Richardson?' asked the boy politely.

'What?'

'You look a bit pale.'

Wally waved him away. 'Yes, yes, I'm fine. Don't forget to back up.' Both batsmen returned to their places.

Amidst unbearable tension, Jimmy ran in and delivered the next ball. It was straight and kicked off the ever-deteriorating wicket, catching the top of Wally's bat just below the handle and popping gently up in the air. Hacker, placed at forward short leg a few yards to Wally's left, tumbled forward but just failed to grab the ball before it fell safely to the turf. Hacker ended up a mass of panting flesh and blubber almost at Wally's feet. Another loud gasp echoed around the ground.

'Bad luck, Lardo,' commiserated the Commodore. 'Next time. We've got him now.'

'He's playing for a draw,' griped Ted Jolly, pacing around the scoreboard. 'What's he doing! Hit the sodding thing, Wally, for Christ's sake!'

Hazel could bear it all no longer, and bellowed out, 'COME ON WALLY!' in her best barmaid chucking-out time voice.

Others immediately took up the cry, including Barney, who for the past few minutes had been dozing by Hazel's feet under the scoring table. He now sat up bolt upright, barking furiously. Henry the stump defiler, also dozing in the sunshine, woke up and joined in the tumult. Cheering began to ring out all around the ground, some sections cheering for one team, some for the other.

Distracted by all the noise, Wally pulled away from the crease and meandered a few yards towards the square leg umpire. He took off his soaking gloves, doffed his cap and wiped his forehead with a hankie. He returned slowly back to his mark, breathing deeply, and asked the umpire how many balls were left.

'Two,' confirmed Charlie. Victor Putney nodded.

Wally had never been a physically strong man. He had lost weight during five years of captivity, and again after his wife died. He felt old, weak, and tired, but amazingly something now stirred in his soul. Hazel's cry had woken him from his torpor, and he suddenly felt his blood tingle, his old heart bump quicker, his grip tighten on his bat. He thought of Janice, the prisoner-of-war camp, and then Hazel dressed in her Sunday best in church with her soft, sweet smile – and then finally, the bowler.

After his previous delivery, Jimmy had picked up the ball and leered at him with a smug, triumphant grin on his face. Wally held that in his mind as the bowler bustled in once again – he would pay him back for that with interest. As he hustled to the wicket, Wally didn't feel afraid any more. Down came the ball, a quicker one, pitched up. Wally lifted his bat higher as the bowler let go, and swung through the line to perfection, catching the battered ball just as it pitched, on the sweet part of his bat, probably the only solid bit left on the dilapidated piece of willow. The two made perfect contact as Wally followed through. Up and up went the ball, over the bowler's head, bisecting the mid-on and mid-off fieldsmen. It seemed to hang in the air for ever before plummeting to earth a few yards inside the boundary by the sightscreen and bouncing into the flower beds in front of the pavilion.

For a brief moment, time seemed to stand still, as if something had disturbed the universe. Then a great burst of cheering rang out. From the direction of the scoreboard, a gleeful group of cricketers, women, children, and dogs began dancing and jumping about. Running onto the field, Ken Kippax, totally lost in the moment, danced a little jig of joy, reminiscent of England captain Douglas Jardine in the Test Match at Melbourne in 1932, when Bradman had been bowled out first ball.

Wally could scarcely take it in. After hitting the ball, he had run a few yards down the pitch, where he now stood in bewilderment. He didn't know it yet, but that instant was to change his life forever.

Suddenly, Cedric was hopping up to him and pumping his hand. 'Well played, old boy.' Jimmy shook his hand, too, somewhat grudgingly. Next was Mellors.

'Well played, old chap,' he said, grinning and slapping him on the back.

What a funny old game, thought Wally. *Only a few minutes ago, he'd been trying to knock my block off!*

One solitary figure, lost in all the excitement, was brave young Ivan Kippax, who was utterly bewildered by all the excitement about him. But his dad had not forgotten him, nor the part he had played. 'I'm so proud of you, son,' he said, a tear in his eye, as he put his arm around the boy and they walked off together.

The umpires pulled out the stumps and the white-clothed figures all trudged off the field of battle. Before he got halfway back to the pavilion, Wally was engulfed by his own teammates, and soon his back was sore from all the slapping. Barney was there, too, jumping up at him and barking, tail wagging furiously. Wally took little notice, just staring at his bat, split from top to bottom, only being held together by the yards of tape wrapped around it. He tucked the shattered blade under his arm as the players clip-clopped up the wooden stairs to the dressing-rooms.

As he passed by, Wally saw Hazel applauding along with all the others, tears running her down cheeks as she blew him a kiss. She mouthed some words at him, but he could not hear with all the noise. Somewhere in the distance, he thought he saw Denis applauding, too. Daphne sat quietly at her table, tight-lipped and almost crying, being utterly professional and balancing up the numbers in her scorebook.

Inside the dressing-room, Wally slumped down on a seat. Ken Kippax came dancing in, fat cigar clenched between his teeth. 'We've fuckin' beaten the bastards at last! Fifteen bleedin' years I've waited for this!'

'Yee hah!' brayed Barry, stumbling inside the door. The others followed, full of joy. When Ted hobbled in, Barry embraced him in a huge bear-hug.

When he tried to kiss him, Ted pulled away. 'Fuck off, you pervert!'

Wally could not join in all the jolly japes, feeling absolutely exhausted.

'Well done, everybody,' beamed the Reverend Christian. 'The Good Lord smiled on us today.'

'Well played, boys,' grinned Charlie, following him in.

'What's up with you?' Billy asked a glum Wally in the corner.

'My bat's busted.'

'Never mind,' said Alf, sitting down next to Wally. 'After today, we'll have a whip-round to buy you a new one.'

'My wife bought it for me, Christmas 1946, and Denis Compton signed it.'

But no-one was listening.

Chapter Sixteen

August 23rd 8.15pm

PHYLLIS

Phyllis Winford-Harvey had been sitting in the club bar for most of the afternoon, getting steadily sozzled, having driven herself to the ground in her white saloon convertible. She sat up at the bar, perched on a stool, like a bird on a twig, cigarette holder in one hand and a glass of champagne in the other. There she held court and scrutinised the local male population which, though she admitted to the barman was not up to much, was probably the best she could get in West Rotting.

Drinking and men were now the sole pastimes of Phyllis these days; anything to ward off the boredom of her dreary existence. Her husband had long since lost interest in her, both physically and socially, and was content to turn a blind eye to her indiscretions, despite the potential social consequences. Despite her advancing years, she did not cut a bad figure in her white off-the-shoulder dress and matching hat. Quite the lady of the manor, tall, slim, and elegant, with long auburn hair curled up at the ends, she looked much younger than she was.

Mutton dressed as lamb, thought Ken Kippax, eyeing her from the corner of the newly-appointed tasteful clubhouse and bar, decorated with framed photographs of players and teams gone by. He was sitting in the middle of the victorious visiting party, who were becoming quite boisterous, as was their habit after a game, but on this day particularly so. They had been well oiled by two enormous jugs of the local ale, brought to them by the genial South African doctor Rorke Veivers. A good deal of industrial strength banter had been bouncing around – most of it aimed at Ted Jolly and his early morning appointment with Lady Edwina. So much so that he eventually became tired of it and left, claiming he had to make a long-distance phone call. The jokers then turned their attentions to the ever-gullible Billy Moon and his lustful eyes for Daphne Charters.

'Go on, Bill, go and chat 'er up,' suggested a very red-faced Alf Fortune.

'Yeah, get in there, Bill,' added Barry Dick. 'She only lives down the road, all alone in a little cottage. You could pop round and ask if she's got any jobs need doing.'

'Yeah, ask 'er if she's got any cracks need fillin',' chortled Ken Kippax. Everyone roared with laughter, Alf cackling so much he had almost gone purple. Unaware he was being teased, Billy just sat there looking bemused.

'Offer to buy her a drink,' suggested a smirking Charlie.

'Somebody lend me half a dollar then,' pleaded Billy.

'Haven't you ever got any money?' moaned Ken, fiddling in his pocket. 'Come on, chaps, let's 'ave a whip-round for Billy's love life – tanner each.'

On another table, close by the bar, Daphne was sitting with Doreen Barclay, gulping down her third gin and tonic of the evening. She clumsily stubbed out a cigarette and immediately tried to light another, but had problems getting a match to flare, which immediately broke up in her fingers. Daphne rarely smoked, except when she was upset, angry, or getting drunk, and this was clearly one of those occasions.

'I need some more matches,' she said to Doreen, her speech now getting slightly slurred.

'But you don't smoke,' Doreen pointed out.

'Well, I'm smoking now, in case you hadn't noticed,' Daphne snapped, clearly in a bad mood and getting more truculent by the minute.

'Oh, honestly, Daphne, I don't know,' complained her friend, looking more anxious.

Daphne leant over the table and whispered, 'Is she still looking at me?'

'Who?'

'That bloody woman!' Daphne tilted her towards Phyllis at the bar.

'I don't know about her, but that big fellow with the glasses keeps looking at you,' observed Doreen. 'He's been staring at you since he came in.'

'What, you mean Billy Bunter?' grinned Daphne, pulling a face. 'He's probably after some more grub.' She belched unexpectedly, covering her mouth with her hand.

'Oh honestly, Daphne. Look out, he's coming over!'

Daphne stood up, pulled another face, and passed wind, loudly enough for heads to turn. 'Oops, bottyburp pardon,' she grimaced, a silly look on her face.

'Oh honestly, Daphne, I don't know.'

'Oh honestly, Daphne, I don't know,' squeaked Daphne, cruelly imitating her friend. 'For God's sake, Doreen, you really are pathetic sometimes. Can't you ever think of anything original to say?'

Doreen visibly shrank in her chair and squirmed as if someone had stuck a knife into her. Daphne was her best friend, whom she loved dearly, but there were times when she could be insufferable, and this was clearly going to be one of them. She was getting drunk, and when she got drunk that meant big trouble for someone.

Daphne burped again, then announced in a voice just a little too loud, 'I need to go and point Pauline at the porcelain.' Heads turned.

She stood up with some difficulty, fiddling with her underwear, so Doreen, wishing to be helpful, asked, 'Do you want me to come with you?'

Daphne gave her a withering look. 'No thank you, excuse me, thank you very much, I'm quite capable of going to the lavatory by myself. I am potty trained, you know!' Daphne sank back even deeper into her chair, her bottom lip beginning to quiver and her eyes welling up.

Sitting at the bar, Phyllis observed this little cameo, a smug grin on her face, as Daphne stumbled unsteadily to the tiny cubicle next to the dressing-room that served as the ladies' toilet. Billy Moon, having got to his feet with the intention of approaching the two women, sat down again.

An ebullient Tim Stewart rose from his seat instead. 'What's everyone drinking then?' he enquired, his deep voice booming out across the noisy banter.

'Pint of your spunk, please, tee, hee, hee,' giggled Barry Dick. Barry often got drunk very quickly and became something of an embarrassment.

'I don't think I can quite manage that,' laughed Tim. 'Not after last night, anyhow.' He wandered up to the bar, exchanging furtive glances with Fiona and Caroline, who were sitting at a nearby table with Tarquin. They had just been joined by Jimmy Catt, looking immaculate in his freshly Brylcreemed hair, cravat, and blazer.

'Do you have a light?' asked Phyllis, pushing a cigarette into her onyx holder. Tim rummaged around in his trousers and produced a battered box of matches. 'Thank you,' she said, in her slightly slurred, raspy nasal twang. Having exhausted the bar's supply of champagne, she had now moved on to vodka and tonics. 'I haven't seen you here before.'

'I'm with the opposition,' Tim confirmed, 'but I only live a few miles down the road. My father owns Buttercup Farm.'

'Oh, really,' said Phyllis, feigning interest. 'I must drop by some time.'

'Feel free,' replied Tim, enjoying the flirtation.

'I do hope James isn't bothering your young lady friends,' she added, leaning close to Tim and motioning to the table behind where Fiona and Caroline were drinking. 'He can be such a frightful bore.'

'Nothing I can't handle,' said Tim confidently.

At that moment, Daphne emerged from the lavatory and began to precariously negotiate the chairs and tables to get back to her own seat. 'Excuse me, thank you very much,' she repeated, squeezing between the gaps, before suddenly doing an about turn and blundering back towards the toilet again, all noted with some anxiety by Doreen, who immediately decided she now needed some help. She rose from her seat and wandered over to where her husband Reg was sitting, deep in conversation with Archie Duncan, Neville Dodds, and the two Mellors.

Since the game ended, Reg had been canvassing opinion from other members of the team concerning that day's shock defeat, which he suggested was entirely due to the incompetence of the captain, who had declared too early, with not enough runs on the board, had badly underestimated the opposition and handled the bowling and fielding poorly. This little cabal were now in general agreement, advocating that Cedric was now a liability to the team, something of a joke, and should be put out to grass in some humane fashion.

Doreen approached them with some trepidation.

'Excuse me, Reg dear.'

'What is it?' growled her husband.

'Sorry to bother you, but I think we should take Daphne home. I don't think she's feeling very well.'

Everyone looked at her with some disdain. 'Why are you bothering me with all this nonsense?' snarled Reg, glowering at her in a way that made her feel about six inches tall. 'Can't you see we're having a serious conversation here? She's your friend, you take her home.'

Something inside Doreen snapped. Sick of being a carpet that everyone walked all over, and tired of being browbeaten by her uncaring husband and even her best friend, she finally gave vent to the years of frustration.

'Don't you dare speak to me like that!' she yelled in a high-pitched scream.' Don't you dare! Who do you think you are? Every week I work my fingers to the bone, making the cakes and sandwiches for your precious cricket, and what thanks do I get? None! I really don't know why I bother!'

The whole room suddenly went quiet. Reg stared, gawping open-mouthed at his mousy little wife, and could not have looked more flabbergasted if she had thrown off all her clothes and danced naked on the table.

'Steady as he goes, Doreen,' came a calming voice from across the room.

Cedric was sitting in the far corner of the bar, well distant from Reg and his fellow conspirators, deep in his own conversation with Jack Hurst and Colonel Bartington-Phypps. But his soothing words had a calming effect on Doreen, who was already feeling embarrassed over her outburst, and now, having turned as red as a beetroot, realising the whole bar was watching her.

Reg also seemed to snap out of it. 'Are you drunk, woman?'

'No,' simmered his wife, 'but I'm jolly well going to be!' With that, she tossed her head in the air and stomped back to her seat, just in time to meet a giddy Daphne coming back from her return trip to the loo.

Up at the bar, Phyllis had been joined by Jimmy Catt who, following some withering looks from Tim and

Phyllis, had diplomatically disengaged from Tarquin's girls.

'Daphne's looking a little past her best,' observed Jimmy.

'If you ask me,' snorted Phyllis, 'she's only knitting with one needle at the best of times. Oh, for goodness' sake, James, make yourself useful and buy me a drink.'

'Haven't you had enough yet?' Jimmy suggested.

Phyllis smiled and put her hand on Jimmy's leg. 'I never have enough.'

'Steady on, old girl,' whispered Jimmy, glancing in Cedric's direction.

On the other side of the room, Billy Moon had now plucked up enough courage, cheered on by his mates, to approach Doreen and Daphne. 'Can I buy you ladies a drink?' he asked politely.

'Yes, thank you very much,' purred Daphne. 'I'll have a gin and tonic.'

'And the same for me,' echoed Doreen.

'May I say how much I enjoyed the teas,' added a well-rehearsed Billy.

'Well, thank you,' Doreen responded, deliberately raising her voice so everyone could hear. 'It's so nice to know somebody appreciates our efforts.' Reg glared at his wife but said nothing.

'Any nosh left?' asked Billy, hopefully.

'Afraid not,' confirmed Daphne. Billy sidled up to the bar, rummaging in his pocket. 'Told you that was all he was after.'

When Billy brought back the drinks, the women thanked him politely. He stood about awkwardly for a moment, not knowing what to say next, then turned and wandered back to his cronies.

'Have you got any cigarettes?' Daphne asked unexpectedly.

Doreen looked puzzled. 'Of course not. You know I don't smoke.'

Daphne rose from her seat again, almost knocking it over, and tottered up to the bar. Sensing what might be about to happen, Doreen was just about to offer to buy some for her friend, but too late, and her voice faded away to nothing.

'Hello, Daffers, old girl,' greeted Jimmy cheerily, as she leaned on the bar, attempting to sit on one of the stools, which proved too high for her, and she slipped off it.

'Twenty Du Maurier please, barman, and a box of matches,' asked Daphne, before turning and glaring at Jimmy. 'Excuse me, thank you very much, but my name is not "Daffers" and I am not an "old girl"!'

'No offence intended,' returned Jimmy, suitably chastised. Phyllis made a show of deliberately ignoring Daphne, quietly sipping her drink.

'Sorry, Daffers, can I buy you a drink?' asked Jimmy.

'I think she's had enough already,' sneered Phyllis, finding her cue.

Daphne stared at Phyllis for a moment, wobbling slightly, her lips tightening as she considered a reply. Back in her seat, Doreen looked on in trepidation.

Daphne found her voice. 'Thank you for your impudent advice. After all, you are an expert, aren't you?'

'Sorry, dear, I'm not with you.'

'Being an alcoholic.'

Phyllis visibly stiffened, glancing at Jimmy. 'Are you going to let this trollop speak to me like that?'

'Er... well... look, Daphne, perhaps you should go and sit down,' coughed Jimmy.

'Yes, go and sit down before you fall down,' scoffed Phyllis.

Daphne was now up for a fight, and Phyllis was giving her all the ammunition she needed. She stumbled around Jimmy and stood face-to-face with her employer's detestable wife, nervous faces all around as everyone began to sense what was about to happen.

'You know,' she began, leering into Phyllis's face, 'I feel so sorry for poor Cedric, having to live with a bitch like you. I really don't know what he's done to deserve it.'

'Go on,' returned Phyllis, a smug grin on her face, clearly enjoying the encounter, 'get it off your chest.' Just at that moment, Daphne inadvertently belched again.

Phyllis grimaced and turned her face away in disgust. 'My god, you really are a fat, ugly, revolting little woman, aren't you?' She looked back at Daphne with utter contempt, then got properly into her stride as gasps came from the now riveted audience. 'Shall I tell you about your precious Cedric?' she spat. 'You think he's wonderful, don't you? Lost his leg in the service of his country and all that nonsense. Well, let me tell you the real truth. He never saw a shot fired in anger. Do you really know how he lost his leg? Falling out of a Shanghai brothel, drunk as a skunk, and got knocked down by a jeep. And as for all this "Commodore"' bullshit, he never rose higher than a lieutenant because he was so drunk most of the time, he couldn't command a tugboat!'

A sharp intake of breath seemed to infect the whole room, followed by an embarrassed silence. Everyone's eyes moved to Cedric, who just sat in his chair, impassive, with his pipe in his mouth.

Still in full cry, Phyllis now stood up and looked about the room. 'Jesus Christ, what a sad collection of phonies and frauds you all are! What's really pathetic is that you all know you are, yet go on pretending to each other. Young James here imagines that he was "one of the few"', Dan Sweeney alleges that he once played county cricket for Surrey, and so on. What a bunch of spineless, weak-kneed excuses for the male species you all are!'

'Phyllis!' implored Cedric. 'How could you?' His face registered surprise, but no shock.

'Yes, steady on, old girl,' said Jimmy bravely.

But Phyllis wasn't done yet. Ever since she was old enough to walk and talk, she had been used to getting her own way, spoilt rotten from the day she was born, and the result now was a cynical, sour, and embittered woman, whose only solace in her middle years was to be found in another man's bed or the bottom of a bottle.

She now turned on Daphne. 'And as for you, you're the biggest fraud of all, masquerading as a woman, you sad, pathetic little creature. No man would ever want you if you were the last woman on earth!'

There were more gasps from the enthralled audience, but all through Phyllis's tirade Daphne had kept her counsel, though her face grew increasing tight and red with anger. She had waited a long time for this. 'Well, at least it's better than being a drunken slut!' she hissed.

'What did you call me?'

'My god,' continued Daphne, up for the fight, 'what a lamentable, washed-up old soak you are. At least I've still got some self-respect. At least I don't drop my draws at the sight of a pair of trousers, actually.'

'You poor, dried-up, frustrated little cow!' howled Phyllis.

Daphne finally lost it, smacking Phyllis hard on the face with the flat of her hand. A loud gasp permeated the room.

She recovered slowly, a dribble of blood now trickling from her mouth, and retaliated with a swinging punch that only caught Daphne on the shoulder. 'You fucking bitch!'

The two women now fell onto the floor, knocking over bar stools and drinks. Across the room, the Rotting Hillers were loving it, cheering loudly and laughing like drains. Everyone except Billy, who had stood up with some chivalrous idea of intervening and coming to Daphne's assistance. 'Oh, my word!' he cried.

Briefly, the two women struggled to their feet, but eventually both fell onto the textured carpet again, kicking, scratching, punching, and screaming fury. Jimmy moved in to try and break up the scuffle and got a sharp stiletto in his groin for his trouble.

Chapter Seventeen

August 23rd 8.15pm

HAZEL

Walter Richardson had not been witness to the dramatic scenes unfolding inside the clubhouse. By nature, he was a solitary man, and though he liked the occasional company, he preferred nothing better than being alone with his thoughts and his faithful hound Barney. The day's events had overwhelmed him. Needing some air, he had deserted the madding throng noisily celebrating their historic victory and sought some solace in the peace of a late summer's evening.

He leant on the wooden rail outside the pavilion, at the end of the dressing rooms, breathing in the fresh country air. As ever, Barney was close by, sniffing about. Wally then became aware of another person; he knew almost at once it was Hazel.

'Hiya, Wol, thought I'd find yer out 'ere.'

'That lot get a bit too much for me at times,' he admitted.

Hazel drew a deep sigh. 'I know what yer mean, luv. They do get out of 'and now an' again, an' that bloody

Daphne's been doin' me 'ead in all day. Fought I'd get some air; don't wanna get too pickled tonight.'

Why was that then? thought Wally, but said nothing. For a moment, neither of them said anything, but just watched the last of the sun going down in the western sky. Then she sighed again. 'It's beautiful 'ere, innit? I could never go back to London. I wanna spend the rest of me life 'ere.'

'Yes, it's peaceful.'

'Come on,' she said, 'let's go for a wander. That lot in there ain't gonna miss us.' She took his arm and they began to amble slowly around the field of dreams. In the past, Wally had always been slightly intimidated by Hazel, knowing her reputation, but not on this night. 'I'm so proud of you, Wol,' she murmured softly, squeezing his arm. 'You're me 'ero.'

They exchanged glances as he feigned surprise. 'Me? I didn't do that much.'

'Yer won the game for us.'

'No,' he said modestly, 'Billy won it for us. I could never have done that.'

'Yeah, but you were there at the end; no-one else.'

Wally's mind drifted off. 'Victory indeed, made us only a little lower than the angels.'

'Wassat?' she laughed.

'Defeat was glory in such a struggle.'

'What'ya on about?'

'It's a quotation, from an old cricketer who lived around these parts, around two hundred years ago, just down the road at Old Farthing Dale, where they first started playing cricket. I think the "lower than angels" bit originally came from the Bible: Chris would know.'

She squeezed his arm again. 'Cor blimey, Wol, you don't 'alf know a lot of stuff.'

'You know,' he continued, warming to his tale but showing off really, 'the story goes that this very area was the birthplace of cricket. But other history suggests it wasn't the English who invented the game at all, and it was really imported from Belgium and France – the Flemish cloth weavers and traders brought it over when they settled here in the Middle Ages.'

She gazed at him in admiration. 'I wish I knew all the stuff you do.' *And what good would it do you?* he thought, rather unkindly.

About halfway round the ground, they reached the old oak tree, under which Jack and the Colonel spent their Sunday afternoons. 'Let's si'down a minute, Wol. There's something I wanna talk t'yer about.'

He felt slightly apprehensive as they sat down on the bench together. By now, Hazel's dog Henry had ambled over from the pavilion, greeted Barney with a bottom sniff in their doggy way, and wandered off behind the tree for a good rummage about. As their owners sat down, she still held his arm tightly, and then rested her head on his shoulder. He could smell her hair and perfume and the crispness of her best summer frock, and it occurred to him he had not been this close to a woman since his wife passed away. A gentle breeze blew her long, black curls around her head, and she gently brushed them away from her soft, round face, something he found utterly beguiling.

'I wouldn't wanna leave 'ere,' she murmured after a pause.

'Why should you?'

'Dad wants to give up the pub and retire. The lease is comin' up soon.'

'So?'

'The brewery wanna married couple.'

'That's nonsense,' he said. 'You and Bert aren't a married couple. No-one runs the place better than you, and anyway, when did anyone care about what goes on in Rotting Hill?'

'The pub was in Mum's name as well.' Mrs. Fisher had died shortly after the war. 'They want a proper couple runnin' fings, not some ol' spinster.'

'Well, nothing else for it then,' Wally said boldly. 'We'll have to find you a husband.'

She laughed out loud. 'Be 'ard pushed to find one round 'ere, and anyway, who'd wanna marry an ugly ol' cow like me?'

'Don't say things like that. You're still a good-looking woman.'

'Ooo, d'yer fink so, Wol? Fancy yer chances then?'

Wally felt slightly wrong-footed and flustered as she playfully elbowed him in the ribs, realising he may have made a false move.

'Erm… no, I mean yes, well, what I meant was…'

She laughed heartily once more, then sighed, 'Oh Wally, I know what yer meant.'

He wasn't sure she did: he wasn't sure he did either. Feeling slightly disconcerted, he offered, 'What about the vicar?'

She laughed even louder. 'Oh yeah, that'll make a good story – the vicar and the barmaid. Anyway, he's only got eyes for Mrs. Ibbotson.'

'What, his housekeeper?'

'Yeah, didn't yer know, Wol? Bin at it like knives fo' years, them two.'

'You're pulling my leg.'

'No, straight up.'

She was teasing him, but no matter. Let her play her game.

He then asked a question he didn't really want to know the answer to. 'What about Billy then?'

'What about 'im?' She seemed to stiffen slightly.

'Well, I thought...'

'You fought what?' Look, Wol, I know what everyone fought. Like I told yer before, we both got a bit Brahms, and one fing led to anovver, and well... I can't 'elp meself sometimes. We all need a bit o' love now an' again.'

'You don't call that love, do you?'

She looked away and into the distance. 'Best I can get.'

'No, it isn't, Hazel. No, it isn't. It's not right.' She said nothing, as if for once she did not know what to say. She knew he was right, and he knew that she knew.

She smiled and looked a bit sheepish, then let out a big sigh. 'Like I keep sayin', it shouldn't 'ave 'appened, and it won't 'appen again, that good enough for yer? I dunno why yer keep goin' on about it. Anyway, why are you so bovvered?'

'I'm not bothered,' he lied. She grinned again, and Wally said, 'What's so funny?'

'Nothin'. Nothin's funny. Look, I like Billy, we all do, but 'e's not quite the ticket, upstairs or downstairs, if yer take my meaning. If yer must know, it wasn't up t'much. I've 'ad more fun doin' it meself.'

'Oh Hazel, really!' They looked at each other and both laughed.

Another silence followed, then Wally remembered, 'Hazel, what did you want to talk to me about?'

'Oh yeah,' she sighed. 'Look, Wol, I'm getting' worried about yer, mopin' about the 'ouse with just that dopey dog. Yer never go out anywhere, only down the Pig once in a blue moon. You need t' move on, luv.'

'I know, it's difficult.'

She looked into his sad eyes. 'Look, 'ows about you and me go out to the pictures next week in Tumbledon? They've got that 'From 'ere to Eternity' one on, with Frank Sinatra. I really love 'im, and I don't wanna go on me own.'

He gazed at in surprise. 'Are you asking me out on a date?'

'Yeah, if yer like. Just as mates, goin' out for an evening.'

'I'll have to think about it.'

'Oh Wol, what is there to fink about? Do y' want to or not?'

He gazed at her again, in a way he had perhaps never done before: this uncouth, unsophisticated woman, probably past her best years, who over-indulged herself and was maybe too free with her favours, yet she was immensely practical and a lot smarter than people gave her credit for. There was something about her presence that was warm and comforting, like an earth mother, sitting there in her best summer frock, being with him and no-one else.

'I know what people fink of me,' she said. 'I know I bin a naughty girl in the past. I ain't no angel, never 'ave bin. I won't tell yer the sort of things I got up to back in London, in the blackout, bleedin' bombs dropping all over the shop. You never knew where yer was gonna be from one day to the next. I 'ad a lot o' blokes, but I couldn't put a name or a face to any of 'em now. I ain't proud of it, but I ain't ashamed of it neither.'

He looked at her earnestly.' But you're a good woman, Hazel. You have a big heart, whatever people might think.'

'Blimey! A big 'eart. Never 'eard that one before.'

'Well, you've heard it now.'

'Oh Wally, I've always 'ad you down as a bit of a dark 'orse. They say the quiet ones are the worst.'

He had no idea what she was getting at but said, 'Alright then. I'd like to go.'

'That's settled then. What about tomorro'?'

'Tuesday would be better.'

'Alright then. Yer should 'ave a bit o' female company. Won't do yer any 'arm.'

'Maybe, but I've never been exactly God's gift to women.'

'Oh Wally,' she sighed. 'You're alright. I wouldn't kick yer out o' bed.'

'That's a ringing endorsement, if there ever was one.' He laughed, feigning shock, then drew a deep sigh himself. 'You're a good woman, Hazel. I've always admired you.'

She leant across and kissed him on the cheek. As they drew away, they looked into each other's eyes, both sad and lonely. 'Oh, Wally.' She leaned over again and kissed him softly on the lips. He felt a tingle in his loins. Was this love?

'Can I ask you something?' he said.

'Alright then, long as yer don't go down on one knee,' she joked.

'What? Oh no, it's... well... erm...'

'Spit it out, Wol.'

'Well, what were you doing at Jan's grave this morning?'

'Wally! I always go an' see 'er, every Sunday after church, put some fresh flowers an' 'ave a little chat. She likes t'know 'ow yer doin'. It's more than you ever do.'

'Can't be much of a conversation.'

'Wally!'

'Sorry.'

'You better ask her then if it's alright for us to go out together.'

'Oh, I will, don't yer worry about that. I'm sure she wouldn't mind. She'd want us both to be 'appy.' Hazel took a deep breath, and then added. 'Y'know Wol, almost the last thing she said to me before… y'know… she passed on, was "Look after Wally for me." She made me promise.' Wally looked down at the ground, tears welling in his eyes. 'I tried, Wol. I said I would, and I will, always.'

'I know,' he repeated. 'I know. I'm sorry if I pushed you away.'

'Oh, it's alright, yer silly ol' sod. We all 'ave our ways of dealing wiv fings. It don't matter now.'

'It does matter. I know you meant well.'

'It was hard f'me, too. I loved 'er, like a sister. We was best mates. We looked out f'each other an' It was 'ard, all them years you was away.'

'I know. I'm grateful.'

Just at that moment, Henry and Barney returned from their chevauchee in the undergrowth. Whilst Henry sat down a few yards away, Barney padded up to where Hazel was sitting, sat down, and put his paw on her knee.

Wally smiled. 'He really likes you.'

'Wally, you really are a wally sometimes. That soppy bleedin' dog knows better than you.'

Unimpressed at being referenced as 'that soppy bleedin' dog', Barney turned up his nose and wandered off, picking up Henry on the way as they trotted back across the field to the pavilion. Hazel squeezed Wally's hand, entwining her fingers with his, looking at him earnestly.

'Like I said, 'ows about me coming over one night an' cooking you a really nice dinner? We can 'ave a proper chat about fings.'

'I'd like that.'

As they held each other, Wally, who was always slow on the uptake, suddenly began to realise what was on her mind. She was right, he had been on his own too long.

'Oo, Wol, you ain't 'alf bony. I'm gonna 'ave to fatten yer up. Come on, let's go back, it's gettin' a bit parky.' The light had almost gone, and the night was drawing in fast. They slowly walked back, arms around each other.

'It's been quite a day,' he murmured.

And it's not over yet, she thought, then exclaimed 'Cor blimey! What's all that palaver goin' on over there?'

Chapter Eighteen

August 23rd 9.45pm

OVER

'Oh God!' groaned Daphne, retching another dollop of blood and vomit into the lavatory bowl.

'Oh honestly, Daphne, I don't know,' commented Doreen rather predictably, as she sat on her knees next to her friend.

Daphne was indeed a sad sight, on her knees in the little ladies' cubicle, leaning over the toilet bowl. Her hair was a mess, there were scratches on her face, bruises on her arms, blood trickling from a cut lip, and she had the beginnings of a lovely, shiny black eye. Her best orange, flowery dress was ripped at the front, revealing her bra and much of her plump bosom.

There was barely room for two bodies in the tiny cubicle, and Doreen's only comfort was a hand on her best friend's heaving shoulder. She felt disgusted and acutely embarrassed, the stench of vomit almost making her gag.

Daphne attempted to throw up again, but this time only a tiny dribble of vile liquid slipped from her mouth. 'It muth have bin slumthin I ate,' she feebly burbled.

'Looks like everything you ate, dear,' sighed Doreen, 'and drank probably.'

''Ave oo got enkie?' babbled Daphne, trying to wipe her mouth.

'No, Daphne, I'm sorry. Here, use some toilet paper.'

Daphne attempted to sit up as she slumped around from the bowl. Tearing a strip from the toilet roll, Doreen tried to wipe her friend's face, which was a holy mess. 'Oh Daphne, how could you? All those people.'

Daphne belched and gagged again, then regained her composure slightly. 'It was worth it; she had it coming. I've been wanting to do that for ages.' Daphne spoke weakly, on the verge of tears. Doreen did her best to sympathise, trying to touch Daphne somehow, but her hand pulled away as her friend belched again, breathing out vile odour.

'You think I'm disgusting, don't you?' whined Daphne, looking up at her dear friend, her eyes sad and pathetic like a naughty dog being scolded for fouling the carpet.

'Oh, honestly, Daphne, I don't know.' There was a little knock on the door, which was half closed. Doreen opened it and peered outside. Coming back in, she announced, 'There's a policeman outside. He's asking if you want to go in the ambulance.'

Daphne didn't reply, then her body began heaving with huge, dry sobs. 'I've messed everything up, haven't I?' she wailed. 'I'll never be able to show my face again. I've probably lost my job as well. Cedric will never speak to me again!' She tailed off into a long, loud yowl, like a wounded animal, her roly-poly body convulsing with huge sobs.

'He did seem a bit upset, dear,' observed Doreen, somewhat understating the situation. 'I think he went in the ambulance with Phyllis.'

Daphne started wailing again, then said, 'I'm sorry if I have ever been horrible to you. I'm so sorry.'

'It's alright, dear.'

*

It was getting late, and the clubhouse was closing. Stumbling down the steps came the remnants of the Rotting Hill party, most of them considerably the worse for drink. Billy Moon put one foot on the top step outside the pavilion and fell headfirst down the rest. Alf Fortune, who could barely stand up anyway, his face as red as a beetroot, and who for the last half-hour had been singing endless choruses of 'Hitler's barmy, so's 'is army, la, la, la, la 'la', collapsed in a fit of hysterical laughter and had to be helped to his feet. Barry was puking up in the flower beds, and Ken, the rump of his celebratory cigar clamped firmly between his teeth, was dancing a waltz with some imaginary partner, waving a bottle of beer in each hand. Charlie was also staggering about uncertainly, also waving a beer bottle, eventually linking arms with Ken and singing a song about power to the working class and proclaiming England a republic. Wally and Hazel had long since decamped to the back of the bus, cuddled up on the back seat.

Only Tarquin, holding up Caroline and looking doleful, did not join in the party spirit. 'Has anyone seen Fiona?' he drawled. 'We really must be getting back to London.'

'Last seen having a goodbye snog with Tim,' slurred Caroline, her carefully coiffured hair now hanging indiscriminately around her face as she chanted, 'Rotting Hill, Rotting Hill, ya, ya, ya, hip, hip, hooray!'

'Oh my God!' moaned Tarquin. 'I do hope he hasn't given her anything to remember him by, or I'm going to be in frightful trouble when I get back.'

'Don't fret, old boy,' chimed his drunken brother, disengaging from Ken and putting a fraternal arm around Tarquin. 'You can always come and live with me and Araxanta if Mama disowns you.' Charlie seemed to find all this extremely funny and collapsed in a fit of silly giggling.

Billy picked himself painfully up from the ground and exclaimed, 'Oh my word, I think I've broken my leg!'

*

Old Jack Hurst trudged slowly across the ground to the back gate, Sutcliffe the world-weary dog plodding faithfully behind, head bowed. There was now a big moon, and looking back, he could see all the landmarks of the area clearly visible. The lights in the clubhouse still glowed as a gaggle of people emerged, laughing and shouting. In the car park, the lights on the old charabanc flared as the engine spluttered into life once more.

The sound of the merrymakers wafted across to where Jack and Sutcliffe had halted briefly to observe what all the commotion was about. He looked down at the old dog, and the old dog looked up at him. It was getting cold, and the old soldier shivered, glad he had brought his coat along with him.

'Eeeh, I don't know, Sootcliffe. Ambulances, policemen; all this foos over a silly game of cricket.' If Sutcliffe could have agreed with him, he would have done, but instead he put his weary head down and shuffled along behind his master. 'Aye, tha's right, Sootcliffe, let's go 'ome. We've 'ad enough excitement fer one day.'

Epilogue

August 24th 6am

DENIS

Visions. Images. Visions in colour; images in black and white. Wally's mind was a turmoil. Images of Janice, smiling. Images of Hazel, kissing. Images and visions of people that blended into one another until they became the same person. Images of cricketers, in black and white, running, chasing, shouting. Cricketers bowling; cricketers batting; first of yesterday's match, then the final Test between England and Australia.

Suddenly the images cleared into one – Denis sweeping the winning runs; Denis running for the safety of the pavilion; Denis on the balcony with the rest of the team, acknowledging the cheers and raising a glass to the happy throng. Then everything was quiet again, and there was Denis, immaculate yet somehow casual in his crisp white shirt, unbuttoned at the collar.

'Well, old boy, you did it.' His voice seemed close, yet far away.

'Yes,' said Wally, 'and you did it, too. Fifteen years of playing the Aussies, and you finally beat them.' His own voice also seemed far off. He could hear it clearly, but the words did not seem to be coming from his own mouth.

'Yes, we both did it,' Denis said, 'in our own ways.'

'I wish I could bat like you,' Wally confessed.

Denis laughed. 'Everybody tells me that, old chap, but the thing is to play it your own way. If you think you can do it, then you usually can.' He characteristically ran his fingers through his Brylcreemed hair, just like when he was batting. His face looked hard and tanned.

'I broke my bat,' moaned Wally, 'the one you signed for me at that charity match in 1947.'

'Sorry to hear that, old boy. Do you know, I used the same bat throughout that whole 1947 season? Borrowed it from someone; can't remember who, for the life of me. Always forget things. Scored nearly 4000 runs with it.'

'Yes, I know,' said Wally. 'I wouldn't score 4000 runs if I lived to be a hundred. To be honest with you, I feel like packing it in now. Get out of puff too easily; can't mend the bellows.'

'Ah yes, old boy.' Denis raised his finger. 'Know just how that feels. Had to pack the soccer in. The old knee was knackered. Still is, if the truth was out. All that twisting and turning.'

'I've hardly scored a run all year.' Wally's voice now sounded even more distant.

'We all go through it,' Denis grinned. 'All part of the game. Remember '50/51 in Australia? Couldn't get a run in the Tests to save my life. Even the Aussies felt sorry for me!'

'But you came through.'

'Yes, but I'll never be the man again I was in '47 and '48. You can never quite recapture the magic. The spirit's there but the flesh betrays you eventually. The knee's gone; it'll never be the same again.'

'When will you retire then?'

'Good for a few more years yet, old boy,' Denis winked. 'Not quite on the scrapheap. Life in the old dog still.'

'If the war hadn't come along, you would have been regarded as the greatest batsman ever.'

'Nice of you to say that, but you know, I consider myself the luckiest man alive to be able to do well what I love best and get paid for it! I wouldn't change it for anything. I've played with and against some of the greatest sportsmen of all time, and thoroughly enjoyed every minute of it.'

'If I get a new bat, will you sign it again?'

'Of course I will, old boy, 'course I will.'

Then he was gone, and Wally was alone with his thoughts and dreams, and Barney was licking his face telling him it was time to wake up. He thought of days gone and the days to come. Ken was right, or whoever it was that said it was a new beginning. He thought of Hazel and their date at the pictures, the nice meal she was going to cook for him, not to mention their 'proper chat', whatever that was.

The sun was almost up, and Barney was barking to be let out. Suddenly life seemed more optimistic. He thought of Hazel and smiled: had it all been a dream? No, it was real.

Monday morning, and time to go to work once more.

OFFICIAL SCORECARD – WEST ROTTING C.C. v ROTTING HILL C.C.

Played at West Rotting   Sunday, 23 August, 1953

INNINGS OF WEST ROTTING

Mr. C.A. Winford-Harvey (capt.) ......lbw......b.Moon................0

Dodds N.D....................c. Stewart...........b.Richardson........21

Duncan A.J (wicket keeper) ....b Stewart.............42

Catt J.M...b.Christian..........52

Hacker P.F..b.Moon..............31

Mellors G.P..b.Stewart...........2

Melville D.M..............c.St.Charles (R).........b.Stewart...........0

Sweeney D.A.N.......................................b.Stewart...........4

Dr. R.K. Veivers............c. Jolly.................b.Stewart........... 6

Mellors M.J...not out..............1

Barclay R.G...did not bat............

Extras: Byes 12, Leg Byes 4, Wides 2, No Balls 1.......................19

TOTAL (for nine wickets declared).....................................178

Fall of wickets   1-1, 2-47, 3-121, 4-152, 5-156, 6-158, 7-165, 8-170, 9-178

Bowling Analyses:

Moon W.	12 overs	1 maiden	28 runs	2 wickets
Stewart T.A.	8 overs	3 maidens	21 runs	5 wickets
R.A. St. Charles	6 overs	0 maidens	21 runs	0 wickets
Kippax K.P.	2 overs	0 maidens	18 runs	0 wickets
Richardson W.G.	5 overs	1 maiden	29 runs	1 wicket
Dick G.B.	4 overs	0 maidens	18 runs	0 wickets
Rev. C.C. Christian	7 overs	1 maiden	24 runs	1 wicket

INNINGS OF ROTTING HILL

Rt. Hon. R.A. St. Charles (capt.) …………b. Mellors (M)…………..3

Fortune A……………………………….…..run out………………….0

Rev. C.C. Christian….…...c. Catt………….b. Mellors (G)………….10

T.P.E. St. Charles………c. Veivers……….b. Mellors (G)…………..22

Stewart T.A………………………………..b. Mellors (M)………….28

Richardson W.G……………………….……….not out………………..30

Dick G.B………………..c. Duncan………..b. Catt…………………11

Moon W………………..st. Duncan……….b. Veivers……………….46

Kippax K.P……………….l.b.w……………b. Veivers……………….2

Jolly E.M. (wicket keeper)…………………...b. Mellors (M)………….8

Kippax I.J………………………………..……not out………………0

Extras: Byes 6, Leg Byes 6, Wides 1, No Balls 6…………………….19

TOTAL (for 9 wickets)…………………………………………….179

Fall of wickets: 1-2, 2-10, 3-18, 4-66, 5-79, 6-95, 7-155, 8-160, 9-175

Bowling Analyses:

Mellors M.J.	10 overs	2 maidens	28 runs	3 wickets
Mellors G.P.	10 overs	1 maiden	38 runs	2 wickets
Catt J.M.	5.5 overs	1 maiden	25 runs	1 wicket
Veivers R.G.	7 overs	1 maiden	33 runs	2 wickets
Sweeney D.A.N.	5 overs	0 maidens	36 runs	0 wickets

RESULT – ROTTING HILL WON BY ONE WICKET

Card compiled by Miss D. Charters

Historical Background Notes

THE 1953 TEST SERIES

ENGLAND V AUSTRALIA

Following the controversy of the notorious 'Bodyline' tour of 1932/33, Australia had won back 'The Ashes' by defeating England in 1934, retaining them in the following two series before the outbreak of war.

English cricket suffered more than Australia from the years of conflict, and the English team that toured Australia in the first post-war series in 1946/7 was of poor quality, many of the players being pre-war internationals who were past their best years. England lost that rubber by three matches to nil and fared no better when Australia visited England in 1948, losing four of the five matches. England did finally manage to win a Test on their 1950/51 tour, but Australia won the other four!

By 1953, however, the pendulum finally began to swing back. England were victorious in successive series against South Africa and India, whilst Australia was now without their outstanding batsman and talismanic captain, Don Bradman, who retired from international cricket following the 1948 tour.

Thus, there were great expectations for the 1953 Test series in England, although, in reality, It turned out to be a relatively uninspiring sequence of matches, played mostly in poor conditions, with low-scoring, slow-scoring contests, much interfered with by wet weather. Len Hutton went into the series as England's first professional captain since 1886. England's veteran seamer, Alec Bedser, took 39 wickets in the series, and in the process became the leading wicket-taker in Test cricket, when he passed the Australian Charlie Grimmett's bag of 216 during the fourth Test at Leeds.

The first clash at Nottingham in June was a moral victory for the home side: Bedser took 14 wickets in the match, having reduced Australia from 237-3 to 249 all out in their first innings after Australian captain Lindsay Hassett had compiled a patient 115. Ray Lindwall skittled England for 144 before Australia collapsed themselves in their second innings, leaving England 229 to win in the last two days. Unfortunately, the bad weather washed out most of the rest of the match, which ended in a disappointing draw.

Australia shaded the second Test, played at Lord's. In the highest scoring game of the series, Hassett and Miller made hundreds for Australia and Hutton for England, the latter left to score 343 for victory in a little over a day's play. Three quick wickets fell before stumps, and a fourth early on the final morning to leave England looking down the barrel at 73-4, only to be saved by an epic, backs-to-the-wall stand of 163 between Willie Watson and Trevor Bailey, holding up Australia for most of the day to save the game. At the end, the home team finished 61 runs short with three wickets to spare, and another draw.

The third Test at Old Trafford, Manchester, at the beginning of July, was also drawn, ruined inevitably by the weather. Fewer than 14 hours' playing time was possible, during which Australia gained a lead of 42 on first innings, with Neil Harvey scoring the sixth century of the series. However, the tourists were then acutely embarrassed as their second innings subsided to 35-8 as the match ended. In another low-scoring match at Leeds later that month, some more stonewalling from 'Barnacle' Bailey in England's second innings saved the home side from almost certain defeat, holding out for four-and-a-half hours whilst scoring just 38, and when Australia went in again on the last afternoon needing 177 in less than two hours, bowled negatively to keep them to 147-4 at the close.

So, honours were still even with four draws going into the final Test at The Oval in August, which would be played to a finish. England finally got their selection right, bringing in Fred Trueman for his first game against Australia, plus the Surrey spin twins – Laker and Lock – on their home turf. In a tense encounter, England shaded it by 31 on first innings, thanks to 84 from Hutton and 64 from Bailey. On the third day, amidst mounting hysteria, Australia collapsed to Lock and Laker for 163, leaving England a target of 132 to win back 'The Ashes' for the first time since 1934.

FIRST TEST Trent Bridge, Nottingham June 11-16

Australia **249** (Hassett 115, Morris 67, Miller 55, Bedser 7-55) & **123** (Morris 60, Bedser 7-44)

England **144** (Lindwall 5-57) and **120-1** (Hutton 60 not out)

MATCH DRAWN

SECOND TEST Lord's, London 25-30 June

Australia **346** (Hassett 104, Davidson 76, Harvey 59, Bedser 5-105, Wardle 4-77) & **368** (Miller 109, Morris 89, Lindwall 50, Brown 4-82)

England **372** (Hutton 145, Graveney 78, Compton 57, Lindwall 5-86) & **282-7** (Watson 109, Bailey 71)

MATCH DRAWN

THIRD TEST Old Trafford, Manchester 9-14 July

Australia **318** (Harvey 122, Hole 66, Bedser 5-115) & **35-8** (Wardle 4-7)

England **276** (Hutton 66)

MATCH DRAWN

FOURTH TEST Headingley, Leeds 23-28 July

England **167** (Graveney 55, Lindwall 5-54) & **275** (Edrich 64, Compton 61, Miller 4-63)

Australia **266** (Harvey 71, Hole 53, Bedser 6-95) and **147-4**

MATCH DRAWN

FIFTH TEST The Oval, London August 15-19

Australia **275** (Lindwall 62, Hassett 53, Trueman 4-86) & **162** (Lock 5-45, Laker 4-75)

England **306** ((Hutton 82, Bailey 64. Lindwall 4-70) & **132-2** (Edrich 55 not out)

ENGLAND WON BY 8 WICKETS

AUSTRALIA

A.L. Hassett (captain), R.G. Archer, R. Benaud, A.K. Davidson, J.H. de Courcey, R.N. Harvey, J.C. Hill, G.B. Hole, W.A. Johnston, G.R.A. Langley (wicket keeper), R.R. Lindwall, K.R. Miller, A.R. Morris, D.T. Ring, D. Tallon (wicket keeper)

ENGLAND

L. Hutton (captain), T.E. Bailey, A.V. Bedser, F.R. Brown, D.C.S. Compton, W.J. Edrich, T. G. Evans, T.W. Graveney, D. Kenyon, J.C. Laker, G.A.R. Lock, P.B.H. May, R.T. Simpson, J.B. Statham, R. Tattersall, F.S. Trueman, J.H. Wardle, W. Watson

Glossary of Archiac Terms

A BIT OF THE OTHER: Euphemism for sexual intercourse

BEVIN BOY: Young man conscripted from 1943 to work in the mines as an alternative to military service. Named after Ernest Bevin, Minister of Labour and National Service.

BINT: Unflattering name for a young woman or girl, believed to be Arabic in origin

BUNK-UP: Rough, unsophisticated sexual encounter

BRAHMS (AND LISZT): Cockney rhyming slang for 'pissed' (drunk)

DEMOB: Demobilisation. The discharge process of civilians from military service

FAG: Cigarette

GOT THE PAINTERS (AND DECORATORS) IN: Euphemism for female menstruation

HALF A DOLLAR: Slang for 'Half a Crown' in pre-decimal money (one-eighth of a pound) back in the day when the exchange rate was four dollars to the pound sterling

(H)OUSEY (H)OUSEY: Old term for the game of 'Bingo'

JALOPY: Dilapidated old motor vehicle

JAM JAR: Cockney rhyming slang for 'car'

NEVER-NEVER: Hire Purchase – an early form of credit, where a customer would pay for an item in instalments over a stipulated period, plus interest

NOT QUITE THE TICKET: Not up to the job. Intellectually challenged

RED ROVER: Early one-day travelcard for unlimited bus travel only

STREAK: Type of powerful railway locomotive

TANNER: Sixpence – the smallest pre-decimal coin, one fortieth of a pound

TELLY: Television

(TAKING IT) UP THE CHUFF: Anal intercourse

WIRELESS: Old radio set

Note: £1 back in 1953 would be worth almost £20 today, allowing for inflation.

The cricket references (fielding positions, technical terms, etc.) are not included: it is assumed the reader will probably be aware of most of these.

About the Author

Stephen Bignell is a retired civil servant and ex-social cricketer living in north London, currently employed as an official scorer for Winchmore Hill Cricket Club.

He has written extensively for cricket publications and websites (see Winchmore Hill Tigers) and his first novel 'The Last Ball of Summer' (about cricketers and the Great War) was published in March 2022.

steviebnotout@aol.com